A COLLECTION OF
SHORT STORIES

Virginia Rollins

D1273185

This book is dedicated to my parents,

Antonio and Maria DiGregorio

CONTENTS

INTRODUCTION

These short stories written by Virginia Rollins (DiGregorio) from approximately 1945-1968 (age 19-42) were found in a bright red metal file marked "Personal File", along with poems and a pile of rejection letters.

Reading through these, those who know Virginia, who is now 94 years old, could see the relationship to her roots, where she grew up, her family life in not all, but in many cases.

Because of this, each story, as applicable, is prefaced with the following: Timeline, Real Life Reference, Sign of the Times and Related Vernacular so that not only her family could see a rare window into the past, but perhaps others with loved ones from that generation, could glimpse the world as it was as well.

PREFACE

How lucky am I, the daughter of Virginia Rollins, finding in the midst of her belongings this treasure chest of stories.....stories that came from her heart, about the times and places of her life. Stories about feelings, surprise, suspense, life. Things that I would have never known about her life as a young woman, a young mother, the daughter of immigrant parents. The woman who stood tall despite her 5'0" height; the stature of a determined soul, seeing deep into her surroundings, her world, as she went from young girl into adult woman. How lucky am I.

DAWD-DONE

Timeline:

Written in 1946 by young adult Virginia DiGregorio (pre-marriage), age 20.

Real life reference:
Dawd-Done was my mother's grandfather, Pasquale DiGregorio, born in Civitaquana, Italy, Nov 11, 1851, died in Wappingers Falls, NY, Apr 16, 1940 when my mother was 14. Came to the United States in 1907.

Meaning of nickname Dadone: "My grandmother told me her father Antonio was called dadone or dadon. It meant a titleship meaning the word Don which is used as sir. It was used as a nickname among friends and business associates." Justinfrombklyn, Italiangenealogy.com

When small Mr Black, the undertaker, took my grandfather down the fourteen steps, out the open door and into the waiting hearse, in my ten-year-old mind I didn't think he ought to have smiled. Not then, with Dawd-done (we always called him that, or sometimes in a respectful, loving way, we called him, 'The Old Man' but not when with him) laid out so long on the brown, sagging stretcher and getting all wet from the indifferent April rain. I only looked at Dawd-done for a split second out of the corner of my left eye because I was afraid of dead people, but I saw Mr. Black smile – right out there in the rain and behind Dawd-done. In fact, he was almost on top of his head.

A day later Dawd-done came back again, all laid out in a shiny casket with white, white satin and candles all around. The first time my mother took me into to see him, I looked at the flowers in the rug and the tip of my shoes so that my eyes wouldn't catch the awful whiteness and shiny candles and brown bed all at once. But then my mother was pulling me down to the soft, furry kneel-rest, and then, very slowly, I looked. The rosary beads seemed aw-fully pale against the whiteness of the Old Man's long, thin, fingers – or maybe the suit was too black. But his mustache was like it always, used to be – full and long and soft. It was the way the mus-tached looked that made me cry so hard. Mr. Black smiled at me and patted my head.

I came in a frightened sort of way, to like the parlor in its new atmosphere – all shadows on the walls from the candles and my grandfather looking so strong and handsome in his big box and the flowers piled so high that they looked like a rock garden – even growing out of the piano and the fireplace. It was quiet and mysterious and if I sat way off in a far corner by the fireplace, I could see my grandfather's face so plainly, all lit up by the tall, white candles. I used to sit for hours and I'm sure that every once in a while, Dawd-done breathed. From my corner, in my chair, surrounded by red roses and ribbons, I could see him. I wanted to tell the other people so they wouldn't bury him by mistake, but I was afraid to speak the words. Just thinking them frightened me.

Late the second afternoon, the day before the funeral, when my mother said they were going to shut the big lid on The Old Man and cover him with flowers, the parlor was empty except for Dawd-done and me. I waited in my corner until I saw him breathe a few times. Then I edged across the carpet, over the red flowers pushing through the dark fur of the rug, to the kneel-rest. I took a deep, deep breath and quick so that I wouldn't get scared and run, I put my hand on Dawd-done's chest and pressed to feel if he was breathing. With my other hand, I felt for his pulse like I saw the

2

doctor do the day Dawd-done got so sick. I heard it – his heart. It took a few frightened minutes to realize it was the pounding of my own heart that was beating so loudly that it echoed from all the walls.

For the first time in my life I had touched a dead person and there wasn't any mistake about Dawd-done's being dead. He could be buried now because he wasn't breathing.

The next day the big lid came down and Dawd-done went out in the rain again, but this time six men carried him. I cried, because I would miss him – and when Mr. Black patted my head and smiled, I smiled right back.

THE LOADED BIRTHDAY CAKE

Timeline:

Probably written around 1963, when my mother, Virginia Rollins was 37

Real life reference:

My brother was 8 in 1963.

Rollins family folklore has it that my mother baked a bad birthday cake but put money in it to entice the kids to eat it and eat it they did.

To this day, my family puts a coin in birthday cakes for the lucky birthday boy or girl, regardless of age.

Sign of the times:

"All the guys were wearing soda cans on their shoes and clonking around the patio": This was indeed a fun pastime, stomping on old soda cans so they fit around the arch of your feet and then clunking around. Google 'Old fashioned game soda can on shoes' for pictures.

"Mike found a dime in his. Tommy got 2 nickels in his.": This was considered a lot of money for a child in 1963, thus the excitement.

Related vernacular:

Keen: "A popular word of approval in teenager and student slang from c. 1900." Etymonline.com

Swell: "In the 1930s, swell became a popular slang term meaning great or excellent." Vocabulary.com

"Aw, Mom," said Joey. "Do I have to have a birthday cake?" He stared dejectedly at his mother's rhythmic movements as she guided the spatula in making little chocolate peaks on the top of the cake. Some chocolate icing dropped on the table. Joey wiped it up with his finger.

"Boy, mom, Tommy Ryan was 8 last month and he didn't have a cake. And Mike Nelson didn't have one at his birthday. He was 8, too."

His mother placed the cake on a long-stemmed dish next to a second cake already iced in white.

"Joey," she said turning to him, "These will be the hit of the party."

"Um," he said, not very impressed.

She went on. "If you'll stop to remember, Tommy Ryan didn't have a cake because all of you went to the ballgame."

"Yeah, that was **keen**," sighed Joey. "Imagine taking all the gang to the ballpark for your birthday." He got up from the table and began to pace around the kitchen.

"And Mike Nelson DID have a cake," reminded his mother.

"Sure, but that was different," said Joey. "It wasn't just an old-fashioned birthday cake. It was 3 feet high and had decorations all over it."

"And it was served by a clown that the Nelson's hired for the day," interrupted his mother.

"Yeah," Joey remembered. The Nelsons always did something really different for Michael. But the clown hadn't been so much. Had made them all kind of feel like babies sitting so still there while he tried to make them laugh. And Mrs. Nelson was the only one laughing all the time. It looked like she and the clown were having all the fun. He had never had to sit so long in one spot in his life – not even in school.

"Yeah," Joey said. "Well, all of us guys didn't think that was so much." He shrugged his shoulders. "At least I'll have an AC-TION party."

"Sure, you will. This party will be loaded with things!" She flipped her apron over a chair. "I tried to follow your list," she grinned. "What's a birthday without a cake? Now scoot – fellas will be here in a half hour."

"O.K. but check the list again," said Joey over his shoulder.

The list was one Joey had made a week ago. It was all the things he DIDN'T want for his birthday. They numbered 8 or 9. Some things that he did want had slipped into the list, too. Number one on the list was – no girls. Then, no birthday cake.

3. No cups – soda in cans instead

4. No paper hats

5. No noise makers

6. No balloons or bubbles

7. No party games – tug-of-war instead

8. No sandwiches – cook-out instead

9. No party clothes – blue jeans instead

10. Potato chips – 2 buckets full

The party started kind of quiet. Four of the boys climbed into the big maple tree and hung there. The other three walked around the yard. Joey began to get a little worried. It was up to him to get things going but it wasn't anywhere near the time to eat yet. Dad had said he'd give him a hand with getting the tug-of-war started after the eats. Maybe he'd better get those going. Tubby Gates had already sat down at the table, somber and waiting.

Joey arranged the short sticks of wood in the barbecue grill and got out the charcoal. A cry came from the branches.

"Hey, Joey, who said you could make the fire?"

"What do you mean?" Joey called back. "It's my job around here – every time we cook out." His father had shown him a summer ago how to light a fire properly. The boys were impressed.

"Boy!" said Mike Nelson. "No kidding? You're lucky!" He scrambled out of the tree to watch. They all formed a silent line watching the fire grow.

"O.K., O.K. Fire's lit. Well what are we going to do? Watch it all day?" said Tommy Ryan indignantly. "Remember my party," he bragged. "Great, huh?"

That was one thing Joey didn't want to remember. Tommy's had been a good party. So far nothing was happening at his.

"Hey, look guys!" There was a yell from Tubby who'd been devouring potato chips. "Look what I found in this bucket!" He held up a bottle. "Bubbles!"

Joey looked and then turned back to the grill, his face getting red. He couldn't believe it. He'd given his mother the list. Oh, she said, the party would be loaded with things. How could she? He wanted to hide. Bubbles at an 8-year-old's birthday party. He'd be laughed right out of town. They were laughing all right. Oh, were they laughing! He sneaked a look. Mike Nelson and Tommy Ryan were sitting in the tree laughing their heads off bombarding the fellows below with showers of bubbles. The ones below were blowing balloons and shooting them at the enemy in the tree. Balloons! Where did they come from? Somebody let the air out of a balloon. It whirred and zipped crazily towards Joey. He grabbed at it and it gave a last breath and shot past his ear.

"Hey-y-y," called Joey. "Give me one!"

The noise was deafening. In the tree, down the tree, balloons, bubbles and somehow or other party noise makers got into everybody's hands and crazy little hats were on everybody's head. Nobody was sitting down, not even to eat. Tommy was on his fourth can of soda, his second hot dog and a half bushel of potato chips. Mike was cooking his third dog and Tubby – they had lost count of how many he had consumed. **All the guys were wearing soda cans on their shoes and clonking around the patio,** strewing potato chips around like flower petals.

"Boy what a party!" yelled Tommy.

Joey felt great. This was a real boy's party. But in one short minute the whole feeling burst like a balloon. Here was his mother coming out of the door with the chocolate cake loaded with candles and prancing horses.

"Woo-Woo," said Mike waving his arms like a bird skipping around on one foot. "A bird day cake."

Joey's mother bounced down the steps and put the cake on the table with a flourish. "C'mon everyone," she beckoned.

Joey could forgive her for ignoring some of the things on his list of "don't wants" because somehow, they had turned out to be O.K. But this was different. Nobody wanted to stand around and sing happy birthday to some old guy. He was right.

"Aw, we don't want any," said Tommy.

"Nah, me neither," said Mike running for the tree.

Joey wished he could join them. He looked at this mother who didn't seem to mind their reactions. At least she wasn't lighting the candles or singing. Tubby sat down and stuffed a napkin under his chin.

"I'll have a piece," he announced. Joey's mother turned the cake around slowly and carefully cut a big piece for Tubby.

"Hey, what's this?" Tubby suddenly yelled with his mouth full. "What's this thing anyhow?" He pulled a wad of waxed paper from his mouth.

"Ha, ha," everyone laughed. Tubby threw it on the ground.

"Why don't you unwrap it?" said Joey's mother. Tubby picked it up.

"Holy smokes!" He shouted. "A dime!"

A dime! Everyone crowded around. They began to grab plates. "Give me a piece! Give me a piece!"

Mike found a dime in his. Tommy got 2 nickels in his. The cake was all eaten up.

"More, more," they clamored. "We want more!"

Joey came out of the kitchen carrying the white iced cake high. He looked at his mother.

"Loaded?" he asked with a grin.

"Loaded," she said winking. That cake disappeared in 2 minutes.

"Boy, what a birthday," said Tommy jingling the coins in his pocket.

"I got 25 cents!" boasted Mike slapping Joey on the back.

"Swell," said Joey happily. "Anybody for tug-of-war?"

BULLY AT THE BUS STOP (UNFINISHED)

Timeline:

Probably written around 1965, when my mother, Virginia Rollins was 39

Real life experience:

Most definitely about an experience my brother and I had with some older kids pushing us around at the bus stop on a cold, wintery day. As I recall, we never told her how the kids threw my brother's winter hat into the road and it got run over by a car, but she must have guessed.

My mother never finished this story which largely resembled what really happened. At the asterisk is where my brother, in 2020, finished the story.

Related vernacular:

Hoodlum: "Popularized 1871, American English, (identified throughout the 1870s as "a California word") "young street rowdy, loafer." Etymonline.com

It was time to put on his coat and leave for the bus stop. Johnny wished he could be a little bit sick so that his mother would say, _Maybe you'd better stay home today._

I'll call the school. But she didn't. She just flipped up his collar, tapped him on the head with her finger and said, "Have fun today, young friend, and tell me all about it at lunch." Then she watched him from the porch and waved him a kiss as he started up the hill behind some bigger boys and girls who walked to school.

Maybe I could follow those big kids to school and then I wouldn't have to get the bus, he thought as the bus stop came into sight. He could see Susie and Ann Sullivan already there. There was only one boy there. Johnny knew from the red hat and baseball jacket that it was Philip. His feet began to drag. Maybe he should have told his mother about what went on every day at the bus stop. But then she'd be coming up with him if she knew and everybody would call him a baby. *"Baby John" has to have his mommy take him to the bus stop.* They would chant it over and over. He didn't know which would be worse.

Philip grinned when he saw him coming. "Hey, Matson," he yelled. "Where's your hat, huh?" He slapped the back of Johnny's head. Johnny's face reddened. He'd told his mother he'd left it on the bus, and she had called the bus station about it. The truth was that Philip had taken it yesterday and thrown in into the street. All the cars from the morning traffic had run over it again and again until it was a flat, blue pancake. On the bus Philip was an angel sitting up front near the bus driver offering advice on how to drive.

Now he said, "Leave me alone, Philip" but he didn't sound very threatening. Philip was his own age but twice his size. Philip grabbed him by the collar half lifting him off his feet. Johnny dangled like a puppet.

"Stop that Philip," said the taller girl, Susie Sullivan.

"Look out, I'll get ya," said Phil. He dropped Johnny and took off after the girls. He took one of the bookbags and threw it into the bushes. He caught Ann's coat as she ran away and ripped off two buttons. Ann began to cry. Philip faced them all and warned as the bus came into view, "You'd better not say anything to the bus driver. If you do, I'll get you all after school."

All day in school Johnny felt miserable. All the embarrassment and chants Philip showered on him were bad but what was worse was the fact that he was scared. He was scared of Philip. Somehow, he ought to be able to stop Philip, even if they weren't the same size. He knew that didn't really matter. Lots of guys who were small could hold their own. He began to think about them. There was Officer Mead. He'd caught that burglar at the fish store last month all by himself and the fellow was at least a head taller than Officer Mead and lots heavier. And how about Rep Romano? He was the smallest guy on the National League, but he blocked like a bull, fellows twice his size. Even his dad. He wasn't a ball player or a fighter or anything like that. He was just ordinary size, but last week he stood right up to old "Money Bags" Sheridan and told him he didn't care how much money he gave to the community fund, it didn't give him the right to own the town. These people. They all had something that gave them the nerve to stand up for themselves. What was it?

That night at dinner Johnny's ears perked up when he heard his day say,

"Met Officer Mead today. Finally got a chance to congratulate him on that great job he did catching that **hoodlum**."

"Wasn't that dangerous to go after him alone?" asked Johnny's mother.

"Guess so," said Dad. "Ordinarily he couldn't have done it, but the fellow would have gotten away and there wasn't time to get Patrolman Kelly in from the other side of town."

"He must have felt awful brave," said Johnny playing with the food on his plate.

"Nope," laughed his father. "Fact is, he said he was scared to death."

Scared. Johnny wondered over this as he got ready to feed his dog. Imagine going ahead and doing something like that when all the time you were scared.

He went back into the living room where his Dad was reading the paper.

"Dad?"

His father glanced over the paper.

"Dad," continued Johnny. "Have you ever been scared?"

"Oh sure, plenty of times."

"I mean, scared but you went ahead and did what you were scared of anyhow?"

Johnny's father put down his paper and folded it. "I guess we all have to go ahead and do something we're afraid to at one time or another."

Johnny's face looked unconvinced.

"See, Johnny," his father said leaning closer, "It's like soldiers who have to fight. They're scared but they go ahead. They'd have to be fools not to be afraid."

"You mean it's alright to be afraid?"

"Sure, it is, son. As long as you don't let it get the best of you."

"Do you think Rep Romano's afraid when he's in a game?" Johnny had his wall covered with pictures of Rep – Rep blocking, Rep running, Rep after the game.

"Well, I'm sure he has butterflies dancing around his beltline. I know I would if I ran some of those blocks."

Johnny contemplated a shoe for a long minute. "Dad," he said finally, "How do you keep it from getting the best of you, being scared, I mean."

"There's no magic formula I know of, Johnny." He put his hand on Johnny's shoulder. "It's just something inside that tells you you've got to try even though you'd like to run...even though it may not come out right for you."

13

"Ok thanks Dad," Johnny said as he hugged his father then turned to head up the stairs to bed.

Once in bed, Johnny lay awake for some time, letting his mind drift from one thing to another. He thought about his father's words and wondered how he could try to do the right thing but at the same time want to run away?

Then, inevitably, Philip's face appeared, and a small knot began to form in his stomach. Johnny again thought of his father's advice and the knot slowly faded away, and he drifted off to sleep.

The next day Johnny walked up to the bus stop feeling somehow lighter, without the usual dread that started the school day, but as he got to the bus stop, he quickly noticed Philip was not there. He knew Susie lived next door to Philip and that her mother was good friends with Philip's mother Alice, so he asked her if she knew why he was late.

"I don't really know," she said, "but I heard my mom say he might be absent for a few days."

"Oh, I guess he's probably sick," Johnny said.

"I don't think so," continued Susie. "My mom told my dad that Philip's family had to leave their father for a few days because he had been drinking a lot and they didn't feel like they should stay."

Just then the bus came, and Johnny climbed aboard. He rode in silence and thought about Philip and what Susie had said. He thought about his own father and the kind of man he was, then he thought about Philip's father and what it might be like in his house and what would make it bad enough so that the family had to leave for a few days? A feeling grew inside Johnny that he couldn't quite identify, but he instinctively began to understand why Philip was so often angry and made fun of him and others.

A full week passed before Philip appeared again at the bus stop. Johnny had not mentioned anything to his parents or anyone else about what Susie had told him. The truth was that he didn't think about it much amidst school and sports and everything else. However, as soon as Philip saw Johnny he marched over and started pushing Johnny around, causing him to trip and clumsily fall in front of Susie, Ann, and the other kids. He even knocked Johnny's new blue hat off his head and kicked it into the street, just like last time.

Lying there on the ground with everyone looking, Johnny was embarrassed and scared. He felt like crying. Susie was yelling at Philip to stop. As he lay there half-dazed, Johnny suddenly understood what was happening. In an instant his father's words came rushing back to him. He imagined Philip's father raging at his son. In the next moment Johnny got back on his feet and squared off against Philip.

"Leave us alone, Philip." Johnny said, this time with all the authority he could muster. Philip stopped, eyed Johnny, then came at him, fists raised and his face in a fury. Johnny braced himself and raised his arms for protection. A punch caught Johnny on the mouth and blood immediately spurted from his lip. Johnny again fell back on the ground but scrambled up as quickly as he could. Philip started to back away, but Johnny ran and threw himself at Philip and this time they both fell back, intertwined and swinging wildly at each other until the bus driver, Eddie, separated them.

"Hey, you boys wanna sit with da goils?" yelled Eddie with his heavy Brooklyn accent, kneeling between the boys with his thick, strong hands keeping them apart until they calmed down - Johnny, with his bloody lip and blood-stained shirt, and Philip with a swelling eye and a ring around it that was growing darker with each passing moment.

"I don't wanna see this again. Now shake hands and get in the bus!"

Johnny extended his hand and looked straight at Philip. Philip, looking at his shoes, mumbled "Sorry," and shook Johnny's hand.

That night Johnny explained to his parents as best he could everything that had happened, even the part about Philip's father. After he finished, Johnny's mother nodded slightly to his father.

Father nodded in return and said, "Johnny, your mother and I are very proud of you for doing the right thing and standing up for yourself and the other kids. That was very brave. You showed yourself that it's possible to have courage and be scared, even at the same time. You also tried to understand the reasons why Philip acted the way he did."

And the bus stop? Well, that was the last time Philip picked on anyone again. Johnny and Philip? They even became friends...

SATURDAY MORNING, SPRING STREET

Timeline:

Written Feb 13, 1947 invariably for a college writing class. Virginia DiGregorio was 20 years old at the time.

Real life reference:

The memory may be reminiscent of the prejudices witnessed by my mother as the daughter of Italian immigrants in Wappingers Falls, N.Y. at that time. Ironically, Spring St. was perpendicular to High St., Wappingers Falls, the street where my mother grew up.

Mom used to recall how when she came home from college her mother would give her a tomato with salt (just like the little girl in the story).

"The clock on the Methodist church at the corner chimed the quarter hour." There actually is a Methodist church on Mesier St., which was perpendicular to High St., where my mother grew up, and two blocks from Spring St., where this story took place.

Sign of the times:

"The ragman was starting up the other side of the street, his rusty bell clanging for the woman to leave their machines, stoves, beds." Ragman: in the past, a man who went round the streets of a town to buy old clothes, furniture, and other unwanted things cheaply. Cambridge Dictionary

Ten o'clock. The sun squeezed around corners and managed to sprawl out over the rocky driveway between the two houses. The driveway was steep. The holes and rocks were bad for car tires. Delores picked up a few rocks in her dirty apron and threw them in a hole.

"There. Play with 'em. There, Mary."

Mary could throw nicely for a three-year-old. Every rock went flying back to her sister Delores. The big cries that came from such a small girl caused a back door to be opened. This was the door of house two, right-hand side of the driveway. A sad looking woman stood there. In her eyes she carried the sorrow and pain for all her people, and in her eyes, she carried all the contempt, smirks, disbelief, ridicule for all who were not her people. Mary and Delores were not her people, but they were "only kids", and she would whine. She stepped into the driveway.

"What sa matter, Ma-ry," she accented the "ry".

Delores. "She makes me mad, always cryin'." To Mary. "Shut up. I'm tired of hearin' ya."

Filomena of the sad and smirking eyes took Mary's hand.

"C'mon in. I give you some tomato. Alright?"

The screen door slammed again and all three entered the kitchen. Filomena walked sorrowfully to the refrigerator, looked sorrowfully for a tomato. The water dropped off the tomato like big tears as she washed it in the sink. She handed her tomato with sorrow and pain to Mary. Mary handed it back.

"Salt. I want salt," she managed to scream.

Salt, tomato. Mary's now. She smiled, squeezed the tomato, flung it on the floor and cried. Delores hissed. Filomena sighed, clasped her hands.

"What'll I do now?" Delores shrieked.

"Well – I guess you haft put her ta bed. That's all." Filomena spoke sorrowfully.

A few cars went by, none came up the driveway. The old truck went down the street just like every Saturday. "Rags. Old Clothes." The driver, the bell calling to the women to bring their rags and old clothes, the truck all creaked with rust and wear of having gone down the same street, the same hour, too many times. The clock on the Methodist church at the corner chimed the quarter hour. A screen door slammed. The door belonged to house one, left of the driveway. A woman stepped out, flanked by Delores and Mary. Her brows pulled until they met over the large, hooked nose. Hands on hips, she resembled a huge eagle.

"Filomena! You come out here. You! I'll show you to talk to my kids like that."

The continuous onrush of words brought Filomena to the door, then outside. The Eagle continued.

"When d'ya think you get the right to tell my kids when they gotta go to bed. You take care of your own."

Filomena's eyes looked disbelieving. She began, "What you talk about. You – "

"You know what I talk about. Listen here you – you mind that big horse daughter of that slob daughter-in-law of yers."

All the sorrow and pain came in Filomena's eyes for the people and the hate, smirks and anger were visible, glowing.

"You no talk about my people like that. I call police and ---."

"I talk how I damn please. I'll show you. You mind your own business from now on."

Two screen doors slammed in unison. A row of shades and windows had gone up at the beginning of the argument. Across the yard, a woman started toward the Eagle's house, still wiping her hands dry on a towel. She was going to fix things up.

A few minutes later the Eagle opened Filomena's screen door. Her brows were crooked, her hooked nose red from blowing. Delores followed her. Mary followed Delores.

"Filomena. Fil – omena. My poor woman. Forgive me. Forgive me," she wailed. She wrung her hands. "I didn't mean nothing I said. The kids, they told me everything wrong." She turned and boxed Delores in. "Filomena, let me kiss your hands – look I'm on my knees. Don't be angry."

Filomena looked sorrowful, opened the screen door.

"Get out of my house. I don't want no fool like you in my house. Get the hell out."

The ragman was starting up the other side of the street, his rusty bell clanging for the women to leave their machines, stoves, beds. "Rags, rags – old clothes. Old clothes."

Eleven o'clock.

THE STORM

Timeline:

This story was written in 1946. Virginia DiGregorio was age 20.

Real life reference:

On the back of the handwritten story, was a note to the college professor from my mother. It read "I couldn't think of a title for this at first. The story is a dream I had just this weekend. It frightened me terribly. I couldn't forget it at all so I thought I'd write it down. I felt it so much that I used the real names of the people I dreamed of. I hope I've conveyed a little of the feeling."

Related vernacular:

bromo: related to "Bromo-Seltzer (acetaminophen, sodium bicarbonate, and citric acid), was a brand of antacid to relieve pain occurring together with heartburn, upset stomach, or acid indigestion." Wikipedia

It wasn't the rain that frightened me although I had never seen it come down so determinedly hard before. It was the water under the bridge, rising and swelling with each new drop of rain that fell until it looked like a huge, dirty glass full of **bromo**, spilling over with foam. From where I stood on top of the muddy, drenched hill, it seemed that the waves and foam were sucking in rather than spilling over.

Archie and Ray stood silently near me. Rain rolled off their hair, their fingers, the cumbersome looks they carried. Their raised umbrellas looked ridiculously useless in the torrent; and as though to laugh at their uselessness, a wind raced up the hill and angrily whipped them from the soaked fingers. Three pairs of eyes dumbly watched the descent of the umbrellas as they staggered, flew, scraped on their way. Archie's clung desperately for a minute to a jutting rock until the winds' prodding loosened its grasp and it again continued on its mad journey. It ended in the sucking foam. Ray's sunk immediately from where we watched. It would've been impossible to distinguish whether the one remaining object was a person or not. We knew it was Archie's umbrella, battling for its life as though some human spirit were in it. It tossed crazily from wave to wave; then, with one last jump, it was swallowed by the watery serpent. Two pairs of eyes closed involuntarily at the drama between the roaring waters and a black object which looked so pathetically human. Archie remained wide-eyed, as though drawn to look on against her will.

I looked at Ray. She was peering through drenched lashes. Without the umbrella, the drops fell on her upturned face with such force that she was unable to keep her eyes opened. I pulled out a book I was carrying. It was a magazine. I put it over her head. It was more useless than the umbrella had been. In two minutes of rain, it was reduced to a pulpy, dripping mess. Pieces of the torn pages caught in her hair.

"---------hurry. Water's up --------bridge."

The wind swept away part of Archie's words, but Ray and I had heard what we ourselves had been too frightened to say. Still unspeaking, we started down the hill towards the bridge. It was old, wooden. I wondered how it would finally sink. Would it be hemmed under by the pounding, pounding of the rain; or would it strain up and up until it snapped under the pressure of the waves pushing under it?

Water below, to the side of us, on top of us. Water, rain –

everywhere. We started across; Archie, first, clutching her books to her as she had been to keep them dry. They couldn't have gotten any wetter than they were then. We had gone just a few steps when Ray called to me to get down on my hands and knees and crawl. I obeyed mechanically. Archie turned and looked at us crawling. She kept walking.

Suddenly a wave slashed up high over the bridge, and when it came down, it threw Archie to her knees. Ray was crawling backwards, pulling my legs to warn me to start back.

We were off the bridge before it broke in two. Archie was on the half that was closer to us. She was kneeling, trying to crawl. With one hand she clutched her soaked books to her; with the other she clung to the rail. Still on my knees on the land, I stretched out my hand to her – crazily wishing it would suddenly lengthen to meet her outstretched hand. They couldn't meet. I saw her eyes, big and dark as the water around them. They were bottomless, penetrating. When she went under, it wasn't the outstretched hand I saw last, but the eyes.

A minute later there was nothing. No bridge. No person. Only angry, dark waters and hovering on the surface, in the spot where Archie had been, I saw two eyes, darker than the water and more bottomless.

Ray and I turned and walked numbly up the hill. At the very top were people. A great many people. And little boys and girls with long, long poles jumping over very high vines – like experienced pole vaulters. Around the edges of the hilltop, some people were walking. A few slipped and were swallowed by the watery serpent just as the umbrellas had been swallowed. And the bridge. And Archie.

I stopped and picked a piece of paper from Ray's hair. We walked towards home, staring vacantly ahead. It was getting terribly dark. I was afraid I'd get lost. I turned and began to run.

I sobbed wildly all the way home.

THE PRAYER

Timeline:

Written Mar 3, 1958. Virginia Rollins was 31 years old.

Real life reference:

I provided the title as my mother had just written the little story down on a piece of scrap paper from my dad's then office at the American Viscose Corporation.

Clearly this was about my brother and me.

The A&P grocery store was up the block from where we lived in Manhasset, N.Y.

Sign of the times:

The A&P supermarket: The Great Atlantic & Pacific Tea Company, better known as A&P, was an American chain of grocery stores that operated from 1859 to 2015. From 1915 through 1975, A&P was the largest grocery retailer in the United States (and until 1965, the largest U.S. retailer of any kind). A&P was considered an American icon that, according to The Wall Street Journal, "was as well-known as McDonald's or Google is today", and was "the Walmart before Walmart". Wikipedia

F inding that it's better with two very small children to walk with a destination in mind than to just stroll neighborhoods aimlessly, I have made a habit of walking to the supermarket with them for a few purchases every day. The children love it and all the clerks are their friends. **The A&P supermarket** is as familiar and dear to them as their own back yard.

One night after tucking in my little boy not quite three, I went to tuck in my little girl, not quite two. Every night I would go through the same ritual of prayers with her as with my boy, however with little responses from her. This time, though, as I ended the prayers, she looked so angelic with her little hands folded that I thought I'd gently try coaxing her into at least ending the prayers with Amen.

I said slowly, "A......," and waited for her to finish it.

Without a moment's hesitation, she looked up, smiled sweetly, and said: "A&P."

THE SHADOW

Timeline:

Written in 1960. My mother, Virginia Rollins was 34.

Real life reference:

I believe the baby my mother was carrying was my sister.

The little story was handwritten on a 4x6 piece on notepaper, labeled "MEMO FROM (my dad's personal business stationery)".

I believe I was the little girl (age 4 at the time) and my brother was the little boy (age 5).

This past winter when I was expecting my third child, our five year old boy showed a normal lack of interest but our four year old little girl glowed with delight, asking endless questions about the exciting event to come and keeping a close eye on the change in my appearance day by day. Fascinated, she would constantly beg to be allowed to feel the baby's movements. We tried to answer all her queries as simply and matter of factly as possible.

One morning at breakfast, yawning and sleepy-eyed, she complained:

"I couldn't sleep all night long. The baby was kicking and jumping so hard."

Imagining that she had probably overheard me complaining too much, I made a mental note to limit the comments I made within earshot of her and brightly said:

"That's impossible, dear. You know the baby is in Mommy's tummy---not yours."

Looking at me somewhat sorrowfully that I could be so stupid, she patiently explained, "Well of course the baby's in your tummy...but the shadow's in mine!" with a little gesture of agitation.

FOUR DAYS FOR FRIENDLY

Timeline:

Undated but probably written before 1968 as the address was still Webster Ave., Manhasset, N.Y., our first home growing up as kids.

Real life reference:

We always did have a dog.

Our dad did work in The City.

My mom was nervous if my dad was working late.

T he twins stood with the big dog between them, their arms around his neck in a protective gesture.

"He won't be any trouble, Dad," said David.

"We promise," chimed in Danny.

"Look, boys, you just can't keep every stray dog or cat you pick up!" Father straightened the blue plaid scarf that mother handed him to wear.

Beep. Beep. Two short blasts of a horn announced that Dad's taxi was turning into the driveway. Dad climbed into the taxi.

"I'm sorry I won't be here for your birthday," he called to

mother. "Sure you don't mind being alone for a few nights?"

"Oh, don't worry about us," Mother said. "I have David and Danny. My two men." The boys' shoulders went back.

"And Friendly," boasted David petting the dog.

Dad snorted.

"Look fellows," he called. "If Friendly can't fit in, we will put an ad in the paper when I get home and that's that."

The twins felt a twinge of relief. At least they could keep the dog a few more days.

The taxi swung out of the driveway. "Remember to take a few minutes in the city and get yourself a new hat and coat!" Mother called.

"He probably never heard me," she said as she hurried inside.

Danny threw a stone at the clothesline. "Four days," he said.

David kicked at a couple of dead leaves. "That's a lot of time to get in trouble," he frowned looking at Friendly sprawled out on a grassy spot happily chewing the handle off Dad's best rake.

The next day on the way home from school, the twins found their four-year-old sister sitting on the fence at the top of this hill.

"You're going to get in trouble, Patricia," said David pulling her off. "You know mom doesn't allow you here."

Patricia took a long suck on her lollypop. "Uh-uh. You're going to be in trouble. I came to warn you. Don't go home!"

"Aw, you've been seeing too many spy pictures on TV," said Danny. He switched his bookbag to his other hand. "Come on. My arm hurts with all these books."

"Better not!" warned Pat in a shout that made both boys turn back. "It's Friendly." The twins waited impatiently. Patricia ran her tongue around the lollypop. "Mommy had to feed him with her new blue, plastic bowl."

"Well, that shouldn't make her so mad we can't go home," reasoned David.

"Oh yeah?" giggled Patricia. "Well, he ATE it!"

Silent, the twins approached their yard. Mother was waiting at the front door for them holding a broken lamp in her hands. Somehow the look in her eyes wasn't the "Come in and have some milk and cookies" look.

The following day, when the boys saw Patricia waiting impatiently for them at the top of the hill again, it seemed like the sun that had been shining so bright had been turned off.

"No details," said Danny. "What did he do?"

"He ate Mommy's chimney broom," she added, "just the sweeping part."

On the third day David and Danny thought about maybe taking a new way home but they didn't. Patricia said only, "He threw up...all over the living room rug." They walked home, very slowly. And spent most of the sunny afternoon moving furniture around the living room.

"Oh, such a big, ugly spot," moaned Mother.

"We could push the piano over it," suggested Patricia.

"I guess it's all we can do," said Mother. They all pushed and pulled the piano away from the wall and over the spot.

"Now, if we put the sofa over here, it won't look bad at all," said Mother quite happily. David began to get the feeling that she enjoyed moving furniture.

That night the boys lay quiet in their bed. Mother snapped out the light and stood in the doorway. No one had said anything about tomorrow. It should have been a great day. Last day of the school week, Mom's birthday, Dad coming home. But over them loomed the cloud of Dad's last remark...." if he can't fit in, we'll put an ad in the paper and that's that."

A large hulk swayed in the doorway near Mother.

"Friendly can sleep with you tonight," she said. "Then tomorrow, when Dad gets home, we'll have to see."

She put a hand on Friendly's head. "He sure can get into a lot of mischief."

Friendly's future didn't look too good.

Outside the wind whipped through the branches and the moon teased its way in and out of the clouds. Inside a quiet fell over the house. Only now and then a great yawn from Friendly broke it.

Something was making a lot of clicking noises on the tile floor of the twin's room. A low rumble began to fill the dark. Somebody was pulling the covers on David's bed.

"Lemme alone." David pulled hard on his covers. "I wanna sleep."

David sat up. A lot of little clicks and a rumble sounded in the room. It stopped, then started again...louder and faster than before. Just then the moon slid from behind a cloud for a moment and lit up the room. It was Friendly who was making the noise, curiously pacing the room, his nails clicking on the floor.

"Danny, Danny." David tugged to wake up his brother. "Look at Friendly," whispered David. "What's the matter with him?"

Danny rubbed his eyes hard to get the sleep out of them. They hadn't seen Friendly like this before. His tail was stuck straight up in the air. His back was arched. The rumble they had heard was coming from him, a strong growl getting louder. He looked ferocious. With a low snarl and a bark that made the boys jump from their beds, he was out of the room dashing through the hall. At the top of the stairs he stopped. He was silent, waiting.

All at once the boys heard what the dog's sensitive ears

must've heard first. Someone or something was picking at the front door turning the knob. From the dim light of the night-light in the bathroom the boys watched, breaths frozen, as the door slowly opened, then softly shut. A figure walked through the house. There was a sudden thud of someone tumbling. The figure reached out to steady himself on the piano. One low chord echoed through the house.

David and Danny hugged the wall, their hearts making more noise than the footsteps below...footsteps that were softly starting for the stairs. Someone was breathing near them. David's neck felt all prickly. He wondered if he could even yell. He reached out for Danny's arm; together they turned. Their mother was standing there, her finger on her lips quieting them and one of Dad's big shoes in her hand. Silently they clung to her. The foot-steps had started up the stairs.

"Friendly," whispered Mother. "Get him. Now!"

Friendly made a slight move. He half turned to get back to the bedroom.

"Friendly, please," David urged. Friendly's wet nose rubbed David's face. Suddenly David remembered his Mother's words..."I have David and Danny – my two men." They couldn't let her down. David straightened his shoulders, pushed Friendly hard and in a voice filled with command he shouted as he pushed, "Now Friendly. JUMP!"

In one magnificent leap, the dog's huge body was soaring through the air. The little group watch wide-eyed as the huge ball of black and white hurled itself at the footsteps. There was a deaf-ening crash as dog contacted man.

In a flash David and Danny leaped down the stairs to join Friendly who was sitting dead center on the man's chest.

"Sit on him, boys, with Friendly!" yelled Mother. "I'll call the police." Quickly she ran down the stairs. "Here. If he tries to get up, hit him with this!" She handed David the shoe.

32

The man huddled at the foot of the stairs wriggled and squirmed and chewed on dog's hair trying to make himself heard over the boy's shouting and the dog's barking. It sounded like:

"No, don't do that...my coat, my coat." Mother switched on the lights as she turned to pick up the phone. The man's crushed hat covered his face and muffled his words. There was a great rip in his light-colored overcoat. All at once Mother pointed to something on the floor and gave a horrified scream that made the goosebumps crawl all over David's arms. On the floor was a blue plaid scarf. The hat had come off the man's face. Looking up at them from under a pile of legs and dog was...Daddy!

Later they sat around the kitchen table drinking hot chocolate and eating cookies. Daddy had decided to come home a day earlier to be there for Mother's birthday. He had wanted to surprise her with his new hat and overcoat and had determined to slip in quietly to hang them up before calling her.

"I would have been O.K. if the piano was where it was supposed to be," he said.

David took a deep breath. "Then you're not mad at Friendly...or us?"

Dad chuckled. "No. In fact, I'm very pleased. Looks like I'll be traveling a lot more in this job and it seems to me we could use a smart watchdog to help out my two men."

He looked at Mother. "Right?" he asked.

"Absolutely!" said Mother.

"Yippee!" Danny jumped and yelled.

David ran to hug Friendly. "Dad," he said, putting one of Friendly's big paws on Dad's lap, "if you're going to be away a lot and Friendly is going to be our watchdog, then I think you two should get to know each other better."

Dad looked at the big rip on the pocket of his brand-new overcoat that he had thrown over a chair. He took Friendly's paw and shook hands.

"I agree," he said.

THE WEDDING GOWN (V1)

Timeline:

There are two versions of this story. I believe it was written between 1946 and 1953. My mother Virginia DiGregorio would have been between 20-27.

Real life reference:

My mother had studied to be a teacher and in fact, did marry late (for the times) when she was 27.

It appears she drew on her experience of growing up in a small town (Wappingers Falls, N.Y.) with The City only a couple of hours away.

Ironically, this first version description of the wedding gown bodice, actually is similar to my mom's real wedding gown.

She married on Feb 27, 1954

Sign of the times:

Jay Thorpe's: "Jay Thorpe was an exclusive store located at 24 – 26 W. 57th Street, New York which opened in the 1920s. One of the best stores on 57th Street, Jay Thorpe offered custom made clothing from French and in-house designers. The store was on an equal footing with Henri Bendel and Hattie Carnegie in terms of quality but had a more eclectic image. Private fashion showings took place in the fourth-floor bistro, where customers could relax with refreshments while watching models stroll by in latest fashions. Wilson Folmar was the head designer in the custom department from the 1930s to the 1950s. The store was out of business by the early 1970s." coutureallurevintage.com

"The Girl That I Marry.": "The Girl That I Marry" is a song from the 1946 musical Annie Get Your Gun, written by Irving Berlin. It was originally performed by Ray Middleton on stage and on record. Hit versions in 1946 were by Frank Sinatra and by Eddy Howard (Majestic label). Eddy Howard recorded a second rendition in the early 1950s on the Mercury label. Wikipedia

Miss Emily Braden was a schoolteacher. What she had gotten out of her 37 year life span she could count on one hand – an A.B. from a teacher's college, a two month vacation every year with pay, admiration from the primary grades, indifference from the younger set and pity from the middle aged and up. She was the town's "schoolteacher." In a matter of a couple of years, she would inherit the distinctive title of "our old maid schoolteacher." Her routine of life had fallen into a pattern as inflexible as her lesson plans for her Senior English class. One Saturday she would browse around in the library; every other Saturday she allotted to window shopping. This was the other Saturday.

Jean's Dress Shop had not allowed itself the luxury of a new after-Christmas window display. The tinsel and the red balls had been removed but the green and red crepe paper still remained, as tempting as cold leftovers from the Christmas dinner. In the center of the window, however, the holiday special display shone forth with real beauty. On a sensual-looking mannequin was a wedding dress, bridal satin, dropped shoulders, bead work from the left shoulder to the middle of the skirt where the bead work held up a tier of organdy ruffles. An illusion veil hung from the beaded tiara to convey the holiday theme, the bridal bouquet was of holly and mistletoe tied with red ribbon. Miss Bea saw it as typically small townish trying to appear New Yorkish and resulting in looking ridiculous but ever since Madame Jean had put out the gown on display weeks before Christmas, Emily had been drawn to the window to gaze almost as if against her will.

Now, standing before the window looking at the wedding gown, she had a sudden desire to try on a bridal gown, at least to feel one on her, to experience the excitement of trying one on just once before the epitaph of "old maid school teacher" became affixed to her. Her sister, Chris had married about four years ago. That was the closest Emily had come to a wedding and the excitement that accompanies a wedding.

Here in town she could never try a gown on. Everyone knew she had no prospects of marriage; she didn't even have a boyfriend. A few weeks ago, the girls of her class had seen her staring at the gown, and they had whispered and giggled about it the following day in the cloak room. Almost as if she were being shoved by invisible hands, she boarded a bus to the railroad station. She paid for a ticket to the city with trembling hands.

"Goin' to the City?" questioned the ticket master.

"Yes," answered Emily curtly. There was perspiration on her upper lip. She felt embarrassed almost as if he could read all over her face what she was going to do. By tonight, everyone would know that she had gone to New York; the ticket agent would make sure of that. And Miss Henderson would give her a four-line write-up in the town paper.

If the train had been any later in coming, she would have given up her plan.

She boarded the train with a handful of other passengers, thankful that there was no one whom she knew really well. She sat alone, not reading, not thinking, just staring out of a dirty window into a mass of snow that resembled bridal satin and organdy ruffles. At the first station stop a woman with three babies got on, a priest and a handful of men, also. One of the men stopped by her seat.

"Is this seat taken?" he asked.

Nervousness and anticipation of her plan had almost numbed Emily. She swallowed and barely whispered, no. The man looked at her, at her restless hands, settled himself in the seat, took out a paper and read. Two hours later they were in Grand Central Station. There in the crowd of people who had somewhere to go, someone to go to, she felt lost and ridiculous. A passenger-seeking cab driver helped her.

"Cab, lady?" She got in. "Where to, lady?"

Where to? She remembered her sister's trips to the City for a gown.

"Thorpes," she murmured. **"Jay Thorpes."**

Inside the store she headed for the elevators. It was too late to turn around now. In the Bridal Department there was one girl before her. She and her mother were glancing through an album at models in wedding gowns. A woman looked up from a desk at Emily.

"Miss Barry will be out in a minute to help you. Won't you please sit down?"

Miss Barry was a sweet-faced, sweet-voice personification of **"The Girl That I Marry."** After the preliminary introductions, she asked:

"And when will the wedding be?"

"In two months," Emily lied. She was conscious of her bare left hand with no ring.

"All right," purred Miss Barry. "Let's look at some of these, shall we?"

Emily had made up her mind. She would look at a few, say thank you and leave. The gowns were expensive, conventional. Emily stood up. "Thank you, but...," she began.

"Oh, just one more," interrupted Miss Barry. She brought the one more out. Emily gasped. It surpassed the gown in Jean's

Dress Shoppe, just like New York surpassed the small town.

"Try it on," enticed Miss Barry.

Emily yielded. In the fitting room she trembled as Miss Barry adjusted the snaps on the hoop skirt. Then she held the dress high. Emily stepped under it and down slid the white satin. It clung tightly to her waist, swept out at the bottom. It fit perfectly.

"It was made for you. Isn't that beautiful?" said Miss Barry.

"Please," said Emily. "May I just look at it awhile?"

It was not a strange question; Miss Barry merely smiled yes and left. Emily looked at the bead work, the ruffles, the train swirling at her feet. She looked at the girl reflected in the mirror as if she were a complete stranger. She stood exactly where Miss Barry had left her, on a square, brown rug. Her zone of virginity. She felt ashamed staring at the girl in the mirror.

Miss Barry came in. "Like it? Would you like to try another on?"

Emily answered abruptly. "No. I don't think I'll take this. I won't try anymore." She couldn't wait to leave, to get away from this atmosphere of satins and veils and girls with futures.

In her room at the "Y", she closed the door and stood in the dark. Shame and embarrassment burned her cheeks. In the empty room she heard the tittering giggles of the sophisticated girls in her Senior English class. She walked to a mirror and laughed aloud at herself to drown out their giggles. Her shoulders shook with her laughter. It trembled on her lips. It traveled to her throat where it caught and ended in a dry sob.

THE WEDDING GOWN (V2)

Sign of the times:

Martin's Department Store: Founded in 1904, the apparel chain spread throughout New York's suburbs in the '50s, perhaps hitting its peak in 1966, when the chain got a feature New York Times. *In it, the* Times *called Martin's an "oasis of calm" amongst the "hubbub" of the Fulton Street square. In 1968 the paper said it did "more bridal business than any other store in the United States," though profits fell all throughout the '70s, and it ultimately sold to a larger company in 1977.*

E mily stood in front of Florie's Dress Shoppe and gazed at the wedding gown she had promised to buy for Mary Alice. The store had not allowed itself the luxury of a new after Christmas display. The tinsel and the red balls were gone but the green and red crepe paper still remained, a bit faded from the winter sun. The bridal bouquet of holly and mistletoe had long lost its significance but the splendor of the gown, the satin and beads and rows of organdy ruffles seemed to make the setting and the not too modern mannequin seem incidental.

From inside the store, Florie waved to her over a customer's head. Her mouth silently exaggerated the words, "Wait a minute." She threw a sweater over her shoulders and leaned over the counter speaking a few words to her customer. Then she hustled from the store and joined Emily outside.

"Isn't it beau-tiful?" she gasped. "Oh my, Mary Alice will be the most beau-tiful bride Creston Falls has ever seen." She pitched the words out to Emily every once in a while, striking one hard. "Thanks to you. She's so lucky to have an older sister like you." Emily involuntarily shivered from the sound of that. Florie's teeth were beginning to chatter from the cold and the wind was making her eyes and nose run. She dabbed at them with a pink Kleenex. "Such a splendid...splendid...giving up your own plans. Why, almost giving up your own life. But you'll see. It was worth it. It was worth it. Mary Alice loves you."

Emily felt extremely uncomfortable. What she had lost or gained from her way of life she felt was her own affair, not something to be aired out in front of Florie's Dress Shoppe. Yet, the tangibles and the intangibles of a schoolteacher's life were somehow public domain in a small town, and Miss Emily Braden was a schoolteacher. Her routine of life had fallen into a pattern as inflexible as the rules of grammar she drilled into her Senior English classes. But now that routine was suddenly being punctuated and punctured by a whole new way of life called...wedding! For weeks she felt herself succumbing to daydreams of wedding gowns and veils and rice. She imagined it was because of her intense concentration on making this wedding a huge success for Mary Alice. Lately though, the picture of Mary Alice was dimming. It was herself she would see...herself in satin and lace and lighting under a shower of rice.

Florie still held Emily's hand patting it and relinquishing it only to adjust her glasses which were clouding up from the cold.

"My dear," she was saying. "So much time you gave...the whole town knows so well...time and love..."

Emily stopped listening. She pulled her hand away and pushed both her hands deep into the pockets of her coat. Finally, the impatience of the customer inside the store released Emily and Florie scurried back to her spot behind the counter.

Emily turned from the window half closing her eyes picturing the veil and gown, the ageless classic picture of a girl in white. She felt herself enveloped in a surge of time. Time gone by. Time standing still. Time closing in and sealing her with the epitaph of old maid teacher.

All at once she wanted to try on a wedding gown, to experience the excitement of stepping on a new threshold. She could never do it here in town with no prospects of marriage which the people of the town seemed to know even more surely than she. After all, she was looking for a gown for Mary Alice. There was no reason why she couldn't try one on herself. They were just about the same size; she could say that the bride was ill, or busy; she could say almost anything. No one would know her. Centerville was only an hour or so away. The one large department store there would certainly have a better selection of gowns than Florie's offered.

At the bus depot she paid for a ticket to Centerville with trembling hands.

"Goin' to town?" questioned the ticket master. "Goin' to spend all that fancy pay you get?" He said the same thing each time.

Emily smiled weakly.

"Look very pretty today. Got good color." He leaned over the counter and winked. "Be careful." He laughed.

Nonsense. Old fool. Said the same thing every time. Her hair as a mess. She had completely forgotten to call the hairdresser to make the appointment that Mary Alice had insisted on for one of the pre-wedding parties tomorrow. It didn't matter. She always washed her own hair; she could certainly do it again today. The party tomorrow would be a big one. Mrs. Lawson, the principal's wife had insisted on having the party and on inviting all of Mary Alice's young friends along with their mothers and fathers --- a sort of economy size family party she called it.

She boarded the bus along with a handful of other passengers, thankful that there was no one whom she knew really well. By tonight everyone would know that she had gone to Centerville. The ticket agent would make sure of that and Miss Lynch would give her a four line write up in the local weekly. She sat alone, not reading, not thinking, just staring out of a dirty window into a mass of snow that resembled bridal satin and organdy ruffles.

Nervousness was beginning to numb Emily. She tried to shake it off. After all, she was only going to town to look at gowns for Mary Alice. She had every reason for trying on a gown that she might buy for a sister who was just about her size. One hour later they were in Centerville. There in the rush of people who had somewhere to go, someone to go to, she felt lost and ridiculous. A passenger-seeking cab driver helped her.

"Cab, lady?" She got in. "Where to, lady?"

"Martins," she murmured. **"Martins Department Store."**

Inside the store she headed for the elevators. It was too late to turn around now. In the Bridal Department there was one girl before her, a young one. She and her mother were glancing through an album of wedding gowns. A woman looked up from a desk at Emily.

"Miss Barry will be out in a minute to help you. Won't you please sit down.?"

Miss Barry was a too sweet-face, sweet-voiced personification of "The Girl That I Marry." She wore a broad band of gold on her left hand. Emily was conscious of her own bare left hand with no ring.

"All right," purred Miss Barry. "Let's look at a few of these, shall we?"

The gowns were expensive, conventional satins. Mary

Alice was small, dainty. She would look best in frills and ruffles. Emily shook her head.

"No. I'd like something with organdy and ruffles. Something girlish."

Miss Barry looked down her professional nose at Emily's broad-heeled shoes, the tight little knot in her hair. "Well, if that's really what you want..."

It took a minute for Emily to realize what the look meant. "Oh, no...", she began to explain but Miss Barry had gone from the room. When she returned, Emily's cheeks were burning. She couldn't explain about Mary Alice then.

In the fitting room she trembled as Miss Barry adjusted the snaps on the hoop skirt that went under the dress. Then she held the dress high. Emily stepped under it and down slid the white organdy. It clung tightly to her waist. Rows and rows of ruffles burst out at the bottom. The lace and bows seemed to cry out against her neck, the face without make-up, the tight little knot in her hair. Miss Barry left saying only, "I'll be back in a minute."

Emily's face burned as she looked at the reflection in the mirror of the bead work, the train swirling at her feet. A silly old woman in a little girl's dress.

Miss Barry came in. "Like it?" She added in a patronizing tone. "Or are you ready to try something...different on."

Emily answered abruptly. "No. I don't think I'll take this. I won't try anymore." She couldn't wait to leave, to get away from this atmosphere of satins and veils and girls with futures.

In the bus depot Emily wanted to find a sanctuary and hide. What had made her do such a silly thing? She could hear the tittering giggles of the sophisticated girls in her Senior English classes. She couldn't wait to get home.

"Sorry, lady," the ticket agent was saying. "Next bus doesn't leave for Creston Falls for two hours."

Two hours. What would she do? Emily couldn't bear sitting still in the little depot waiting and leafing through magazines. She left the depot and began to walk, thankful that there was no one she knew around. If she could preoccupy herself with something perhaps the shame and embarrassment she felt wouldn't burn so much. Across the street was an ultra-modern beauty salon. Emily touched her hair. Maybe she could get it done now, here. Then Mary Alice wouldn't be disappointed in her for not getting it set.

Emily walked in and waited at the shiny desk. It was a big, busy place. The receptionist found an operator to take care of Emily. It was a blonde. She looked Emily over from head to toe. As she combed out the tight knot, she fingered Emily's long hair.

"Got some wave here, Ma'am. Bet this would look nice cut short."

Emily shook her head. "Oh, no," she said. "I've always had long hair."

"Well, then...maybe it's time for a change," answered the blonde as she wrapped a towel around Emily's hair.

Time for a change. There would be many changes now. Mary Alice would be gone in a few weeks. There would be no need for all the rooms now so she would probably sell the house. It would be lonely. Mary Alice had filled the house with jumping music and noise and young people. She didn't want to think about that or the wedding gown that looked so ludicrous.

"Cut it", she said sharply. The blonde girl turned. Emily spoke somewhat sadly. "Maybe it is time for a change."

The bus was ready at the depot when Emily crossed the street. It was already quite crowded. She hurried to get a seat glancing quickly around to see if there was anyone she knew. This time she was hoping there was. There was the color of excitement in her cheeks and her eyes were brilliant. Emily smiled to herself as she looked at her manicured nails. She had often read about how a new hat or a new hairdo could raise your spirits, but she hadn't really ever given herself a chance to find out. It was quite dark outside now and as Emily looked through the window, she saw her reflection. The girl looking back at her looked young, her hair looked casually windblown and soft. The lights shining from the ceiling of the bus brought out shining highlights in the waves and curls. Emily felt suddenly young and carefree.

As the driver started the motor one last passenger got on. Emily looked up as he handed the driver his ticket. As he turned and started down the aisle, she recognized him. Betty Henderson's Dad. Betty was a senior last year along with Mary Alice. Her mother had died, after a long illness, during the summer before the beginning of Betty's Senior year. Emily had meant to call on Betty and her Dad but in the rush of the start of a new school year she had neglected it. Mr. Henderson looked at her as he passed her seat, then went on. He hadn't even recognized her.

"Why, it's you...Miss Braden, I mean." He had turned around and was standing by her seat. "I...I didn't recognize.... well, that is, you're looking wonderful, Miss Braden. May I join you?"

Emily moved over in the seat. He was looking steadily at her with very interested gray eyes. She mumbled some words about shopping and the weather.

"Well," he went on. "I see there will be a wedding in your family soon. We're looking forward to going to the Lawson's party tomorrow."

Emily turned very quickly. "Oh, will you be there at the party too?" All at once she felt flushed and embarrassed. "That is...I mean, you and Betty."

He smiled. His eyes were really very warm and gray.

"Yes. Then we'll be getting started on Betty. My other two children are married, and Betty will be the third time around for me."

Emily looked out the window. The third time around. The

phrase reached out to Emily. Inside she could hear herself saying...it's time for a change... A decision suddenly swept through her and turned her around. She smiled very brightly.

"Well, Mary Alice will be going on ahead with her fiancé, but I'll be going, too. It's the first time around for me."

"Betty's going on ahead with some of her gang. Say, why don't I pick you up. We could join forces, so to speak. Would you like that?"

Emily took a quick look at the girl reflected in the window. She still looked very good. No one had looked at her like Mr. Henderson was looking at her now in a long time. She turned to him and her smile didn't fade one bit.

"Yes," she said. "I'd like that. Very much."

A FAT PART FOR CATHY

Timeline:

Probably written in 1946 as there is evidence of someone editing this, perhaps a college teacher. Virginia DiGregorio was 20 years old.

Real life reference:

Not sure the basis for the story although it does show the insecurities of a young girl, common to most of us.

Cathy grabbed her raincoat from the front hall closet and covered the large paper bag she was carrying with it. Her Mother's voice called form the dining room. "Breakfast time." The smell of bacon and sausages was tantalizing. From the hall Cathy could see Aunt Milly's broad back at the stove and a stack of pancakes keeping warm on a hot tray. "Why couldn't this be tomorrow's breakfast?" she muttered hating herself for her three weaknesses .... breakfast, lunch, and dinner. Out loud she called, "Can't, Mom. Have to run."

"No breakfast? Don't you feel well?" Mother came out into the hall. "A raincoat, Cathy? It's 80 degrees out!"

"Ummmm", answered Cathy. Well, it may rain." She was off blowing a kiss and calling over her shoulder, "Try-outs today. May be late. Barbara's waiting."

Barbara was sauntering across the lawn. "Hi!" she called

sniffing the air. "Let's go see what's delicious inside."

"Not today." Cathy pulled at her arm and steered her up the hill.

"It's not fair, Cathy," said Barbara as they stopped to watch a woman arrange freshly baked coffeecakes in the bakery window. "Just 'cause you haven't been eating for a week. Why did you have to go on a diet just when your Aunt Milly's visiting?"

"Best time," smiled Cathy. "She's a good reminder of why I shouldn't eat too much." Cathy pulled the paper bag from under the raincoat. "This will be another reminder," she said.

"What's in there?" asked Barbara curiously.

"Show you after school." Cathy kicked a stone ahead of her on the sidewalk. "I'm worried about the try-outs. I don't want to get that part."

"No problem," said Barbara. "Just don't go. If it annoys you that Pete Henderson asked you and Tootsie McMann to try out for the fat girl's part, just don't go. I wouldn't."

"I'll bet you wouldn't," replied Cathy. "Pete Henderson asked me, not you."

Barbara squealed. "Imagine. The Captain of the Midget League asking you to do something. You bet I'd do anything. Sell tickets, sweep the floor, carry his books." She did a little dance step in excitement.

Cathy shifted her books as they waited for the light to change. Ahead was the school. Not too far away would be 3:00 and try-outs. Pete Henderson as the student director of the play had singled her out to play a part, at least try out for it. She knew that he had because of her size and she didn't like thinking about it. If she didn't go to the try-outs, she probably wouldn't get another chance like this to get to know Pete better. If she did go, and got the part, it would be like announcing to the world, "Fat Girl."

"Of course," suggested Barbara, "Tootsie may get it. But on

the other hand, you read better."

"It's not a speaking part," said Cathy. "That's what makes it so awful. They are just supposed to look at me and laugh."

Her mother had spoken to her later in the kitchen as they washed the dishes. "There's nothing wrong in not being small or thin," she said. "People like us for what we are. Be yourself." She had touched Cathy's brown hair. "You have nice, shiny, long hair and a beautiful smile. Those are two good points in your favor, and you should make the most of what you have. Besides," she had added untying her apron, "it's having something in common that brings people together."

The first bell rang, and the girls joined the push of students in the last-minute scurry for seats before morning prayers. "Meet me in the girl's room after school," Cathy whispered to Barbara. "I have a plan."

The day began with the inevitable spelling test and dragged through an assortment of what seemed to Cathy impossibly dull demands. Finally, a measured tick of the clock set off the bell. School was out.

Cathy waited until the last few stragglers had trickled from the hall and then she pulled the paper bag from her desk. In the washroom she laughed out loud as Barbara looked inside the bag and gasped.

"Haven't you ever seen a corset before?" she giggled. She pulled out the white satiny elasticized object. "It's boned," she said. She held it up in front of her. "See, it laces and ties here," she flipped aside a panel, "and there are hooks and eyes here." The object looked like it could stand up straight without anyone in it.

Barbara finally managed to speak. "It's Aunt Milly's," she said superfluously. "Will it work?"

Cathy nodded as she began to unfasten the skirt. "Give me a hand. O.K. Barbara?"

"Take your socks off, too," volunteered Barbara. "Always

makes your legs look
slimmer."

When the girls slipped into their seats in front of the auditorium, there were already about 20 other hopeful aspirants waiting. The back was darkened somewhat by the closed doors and draped windows, but this hadn't discouraged anyone. The back seats were filled with giggling girls. A few bolder boys were sitting halfway down to the front, legs stretched over the seats in front of them. The drama teacher stood up to take roll call.

"Where is Tootsie McMann?" she asked.

One of the boys in the middle of the auditorium called out, "She didn't want to try out for that part. Said she doesn't like to be typed." Everyone laughed. Cathy's heart sank. She'd be the only one trying out now. The drama teacher called the group to attention.

"We'll begin in just about fifteen minutes. Just be patient. And let me advise you on one point," she emphasized, "Make the most of what you have to make the character real. It makes for an honest portrayal."

Cathy sat uncomfortably tall and straight, imprisoned in Aunt Milly's corset. The auditorium was too warm, and the air was stifling. That contraption was murder. Then she began to realize that maybe it wasn't just the corset that was causing discomfort. It was the picture she was seeing of herself that was the most uncomfortable. Mother had said, "Be yourself." Tootsie had ridiculously said that she didn't want to be typed. Tootsie hadn't been able to put her pride to the test. And here she was hiding hers in all sorts of subterfuges of corsets and stockingless feet. Cathy stood up. "Be right back," she whispered to Barbara as she left the auditorium through the side door.

In the washroom she quietly put on her socks. She unfastened her skirt and with some difficulty untied the laces and unhooked the eyes to Aunt Milly's corset. She carried the bag with her into the auditorium. "Be honest in your portrayal," the drama teacher had said. She had really been echoing her Mother's words.

Cathy knew that she looked the same when she went up on the stage, but she also knew that inside she had changed a little bit towards growing up from all this. She smiled brightly when Pete Henderson said, "You'll do fine for the part, Cathy."

When she went back to her seat to pick up her raincoat and bag, the drama teacher called her.

"Cathy," she said. "Pete's going to need some help in coaching these lines and since you don't have a speaking part, I wonder if you'd mind helping him?"

Cathy glanced at Pete and he flashed a smile of relief at her. Well, it was a start anyhow. They'd be working together. And as Mother had said, "It's having something in common that brings people together."

After all, thought Cathy, who knows how this might end?

FAREWELL TO GRANDPA

Timeline:

Undated but probably written prior to 1968 as the Webster Ave., Manhasset, New York address was typed on the story. My mother Virginia Rollins was probably in her early 40's.

Real life reference:

This clearly is about my mother's memories of growing up with an extended family. This is about her grandfather, Pasquale DiGregorio, notably as the description of the mustache aptly fits the pictures I have.

The underground winter house, the smell of the grapes crushed for wine – even I have those memories of her home when we would visit Wappingers Falls. The musty smell of wine in the basement...How impressionable are the memories of our families on our lives...

That year September and Grandpa walked hand in hand, more gloriously, more deliberately, with more dignity than ever before. That year Grandpa worked harder on the workdays. He cleaned out the barns, pulled out the bean poles, cut down the rotting apple tree so that it wouldn't have to suffer another winter. On Monday through Friday he picked apples and laid them gently, one by one, in the bushel baskets and then put the baskets in twos on the wheelbarrow. He must have made at least eight trips with the wheelbarrow to the underground winter house where apple smell mingled with cabbage smell. He washed the wine barrels with more care that year, rubbing them vigorously with a long-handled brush and swashing the water around so hard it would splash out and wet all the sidewalk. After rubbing down five or six such barrels he entered the house surrounded by a faint odor of diluted wine... like the odor of bottom-of-the-barrel wine that's been left standing for some time. Later, there would be the smell of ripe grapes on him from the grapes that he had pressed in the barns, using the pressing machine that had become stained by blue juice flowing over and in it for the past thirty years. For a few days Grandpa's hands would be stained from the juice that had flowed over them. The blue clung to the veins that stood out on his heavy, long hands making them all the more visible and unforgettable.

On Saturdays Grandpa dressed with more than the usual care. His fine black suit he laid out Friday night but waited until the next morning to brush it carefully in the pure daylight, not trusting the glare of the electric bulb. And he's rubbed the black shoes with the same strength that he had rubbed the wine barrels until they reflected the patches of sun that shone on them where they sat on the windowsill. By nine o'clock Grandpa would be ready, starched collar, black tie, grey hat, sweeping white mustache. His strong fingers clasped a cane which he swung, touching the ground with it only occasionally to beat a short rhythm as he waited at street corners. At one o'clock Grandpa would come home, collar still starched, shoes only slightly powdered with dust and his mustache suspiciously shorter, his cheeks a bright, delicate pink where the barber had just shaved them. That year his eyes seemed to be even bluer as they watched the activity of eager hands searching the Hershey bars and other presents in his pockets. And those Saturday nights the stories that he told week after week would live freely, wonderfully new again in the freshness and strength of his voice...

And it was in that year that Grandpa began to slow up, and

when his sharp blue eyes missed some specks on the dark suit it was noticeable, as noticeable as the brilliant gold of the leaves that lined the paths of the park where he walked, a gold silently, unobtrusively turning to a subdued brown. That year when Grandpa's voice trailed off in the stories and the blue eyes looked off into distances his listeners did not know, they only waited. Grandpa...old men...walk in dreams, brown as September, final as the harvest. Old men and September die slow.

THE UNHAPPY
SCARECROW

Timeline:

Undated but probably written before 1968 as the address was still Webster Ave., Manhasset, N.Y., our first home growing up as kids.

Real life reference:

Reminiscent of country living, much as the environment my mother grew up in coupled with the loving experience of parent and child, certainly what she was experiencing at this time in her life with our family while she was in her early forties.

Signs of the time:

Derby hat: "A derby, as the distinctive round hat with a little brim, was made in the U.S. in the 1850s, but it's probably named after the Derby horse race in England, where men wore this kind of hat. The race was named after the 12th Earl of Derby." Vocabulary.com

Related vernacular:

Gay: "Adjective, (dated) lighthearted and carefree" Dictionary.com

Far off in the country there was a lovely green garden with rows and rows of green vegetables stretching out as far as you could see. And right in the middle of this lovely garden there stood a scarecrow. He was not very beautiful. In fact, he was not pretty at all. He had been put together in a hurry one day when Farmer Black had wanted to frighten away the birds that were eating his plants. The scarecrow wore an old plaid shirt that was all dirty, ragged blue jeans and an old **derby hat**. He had no hair, no eyes, no nose, and no ears.... just a mouth. Farmer Black really had no imagination at all. He had taken a black crayon and drawn a mouth, a mouth that dropped at the corners and that looked so very sad. He was a most unhappy looking scarecrow.

The sad old scarecrow stood out in the garden many days and many nights. Some days he was drenched with rain. Other days he almost baked in the sun. At last, Farmer Black took him out of the garden and threw him aside. He was forgotten.

One day Farmer Black's granddaughter came from the city with her Mommy and Daddy to visit the farm. Her name was Mary Anne. Mary Anne loved the farm and she looked into every corner every time she visited. And that is how she found the scarecrow.

"Oh, Daddy," she cried as she pulled him to the spot where the scarecrow lay. "Look at how sad he is. See how his mouth droops. And his clothes are so dirty. I should like very much to fix him up."

Mary Anne's mother, who had come running to see, looked at the old scarecrow and frowned. He was really not very pretty.

"What on earth would you do with him, Mary Anne?" she said. "Now put him away."

But Mary Anne pleaded and pleaded and so when she and her family left the farm, who was sitting in the back seat of the car but the old scarecrow.

Mary Anne's Daddy was very kind and clever. He helped Mary Anne straighten the broken legs and put them on a nice sturdy base. They set the scarecrow, right in Mary Anne's room. There he was surrounded by beautiful dolls and great big furry dogs and all the frilly things little girls have. Mary Anne's Mommy washed the old plaid shirt and mended the holes. Mary Anne brushed and brushed the old derby hat until it was quite shiny. Best of all, she glued on Mr. Scarecrow a beautiful head of yarn and gave him her Daddy's bow tie. Daddy didn't mind at all. They then put a pair of **gay** red corduroy trousers over his wooden legs. He was probably the best dressed scarecrow in all the world...and the cleanest.

"Now," said Mary Anne, "if he had eyes, he could see me. He could watch over me at night while I'm sleeping, and he wouldn't look so sad." So, she gave him two button eyes, but he still looked sad. "Oh, if he had ears, he could hear me when I talk to him." So, she gave him two medium sized ears. "He should have a nose to balance his face," Mary Anne said, so she gave him a button for a nose. "I know," she cried. "I'll give him a smiling mouth. It will turn way up at the corners." Which it did.

Now Mr. Scarecrow could look out the window and look and look and look. At last he could see Mary Anne and the trees, the sky, and the sun. Now he could hear the sounds of the cars and could hear Mary Anne's laugh. He could even smell the lovely perfume Mary Anne's mother wore and the smoke from Daddy's pipe. And no wonder he smiled.

Mary Anne was so thrilled. She clapped her hands and cried, "I love you my scarecrow. I love you! You are a real friend."

Life couldn't have been better. And it didn't matter that he couldn't talk because Mary Anne never stopped talking for him to answer anyway. Mary Anne was very happy for quite a while but then one day she became quite sad. She sat quietly in the big chair while her mother sewed.

"What is it Mary Anne," asked Mommy. "Aren't you happy?"

"Oh Mommy," said Mary Anne, "It's my friend, Mr. Scarecrow. I love him so much. Like I love you and Daddy, and it makes me feel good right here." She pointed to her heart. "But Mommy," Mary Anne's eyes got very wide. "Mr. Scarecrow doesn't have a heart."

Mary Anne's Mommy stopped sewing for a while and thought. Then she said, "Mary Anne, go get Mr. Scarecrow."

Mary Anne ran to her room and brought out her smiling friend.

Mommy took a bright red cloth from her sewing basket. She took her scissors and made a heart. Then, very carefully, she sewed it on him. Immediately all the love that Mr. Scarecrow felt inside just overflowed. Now he was the happiest scarecrow in the world.

CHOO CHOO GOES
TO A WEDDING

Timeline:

Most likely written around 1967. Virginia Rollins was 41.

Real life reference:

We did have a cat, but nothing like Choo Choo!

Sign of the times:

"I Love You Truly": "I Love You Truly" is a parlor song written by Carrie Jacobs-Bond. Since its publication in 1901 it has been sung at weddings, recorded by numerous artists over many decades, and heard on film and television. Wikipedia

C hoo Choo was a Sunday kind of cat. He liked to go to church. Of course, he liked to go to church because it was great fun to chase Church Mouse. Also, Choo Choo liked to go to weddings. Most of all he liked to jump on the bride's shiny dress and ride down the aisle on the bride's long train. No one else liked that too much, especially the bride.

Antonio was an everyday kind of boy. He liked to go to church because it was great fun to play with Choo Choo. Also, he liked weddings. Especially, he liked to catch the pennies people threw at the bride for good luck.

Papa John was a special kind of priest. He liked to go to church because church is where priests mostly live. Papa John liked weddings. He liked Antonio and Choo Choo. Papa John liked everybody. So, they were all happy.

But then... it was at a wedding one day in June when no one should be sad. The organ was playing wedding music. A lady in a pink-petuny hat was singing "**I Love You Truly.**" At first Antonio only heard the music. Then he thought he heard "meow." He shook his head hard when he saw the cat. He was sitting proud and tall on the bride's long, satin train. His tail curled like a ring around him. His sassy smile stretched a mile as he glided down the aisle. Everyone else saw him. They all covered their mouths and laughed.

The bride's Mama was very angry. The bride's godmother shook her finger and said, "Spoiled cat! Good for nothing cats don't belong in church!"

Papa John said, "No more cats at weddings." He also said, "But cats and boys are always welcome - after the wedding."

Antonio called the cat. "Here, kitty. Here, kitty."

"Every creature of God should have a name," said Papa John after the wedding. Antonio thought about it as he stroked the cat's head. "Too bad you like to ride trains, little creature."

"Yes," said Antonio. "He likes to ride trains."

"So, let's call him Choo Choo," said Papa John.

It was a ding-dong kind of Sunday. All the bells were going "ding-dong" because there was going to be a wedding. The organ was playing wedding music. The church was full of people and flowers. All the people inside kept looking outside. A man with a big camera kept running up and down the stairs. Antonio and Choo Choo peeked inside. Oh, how they wanted to go to the wedding.

A big black car pulled up. Out stepped the Bride, all dressed in white. A second big, black car pulled up. Out stepped the bridesmaids, all dressed in blue. Another big, black car pulled up. Out stepped the Bride's Mommy and Daddy, all puffed and shouting:

"Keep that cat OUT OF CHURCH!"

In the hall in the back of the church, the Bridesmaids fixed their hats. The Bride fixed her veil. The music boomed: "HERE COMES THE BRIDE! HERE COMES THE BRIDE!"

All at once the bridesmaids screamed and jumped on the table. The bride screamed and jumped into her Daddy's arms. All the people stood up. Papa John came running down the aisle. Antonio and Choo Choo sneaked inside to take a look. There was Church Mouse, poised in the center of the hall. He polished his whiskers, then...! Up the table leg he scurried. Down the bridesmaid's ribbons he slid.

"Help!" screamed the Bride.

"EEEEEEEKKK!" screamed the Bridesmaids. The Bride's Mommy nearly fainted.

"Do something!" yelled the Daddy. He spied Antonio. "The Cat! The Cat! Get the Cat!"

"Goll......y!" said Antonio

"Charge, Choo!" ordered Papa John. Choo Choo zipped from Antonio's arms. Church Mouse ran. He squeaked around the pews and squeezed under seats. All the ladies stood on the seats. Choo ran after him. Up the stairs. Down the stairs. To the choir loft. Behind the organ. Choo Choo took a giant jump. Ppfft...! That was the end of Church Mouse.

"Hurray for Choo!" cried all the people.

"Good cat," said the Daddy.

Antonio stood very proud. The Bride stuck a white flower in his buttonhole. The littlest Bridesmaid tied a blue ribbon on Choo Choo's collar. The Bride's Mommy took Antonio's hand. Choo Choo walked in front with this head very high. All together they marched to the very first pew.

A lady in a frilly-fruity hat sang, "Here Comes the Bride."

Down the aisle came the Bride. She looked very beautiful. At her side was her Daddy. He looked very nervous. At the altar was Papa John. He looked very serious. In the first pew was the Bride's Mommy. She looked very weepy. And in the pew with her sat Antonio and Choo. They looked very happy.

SCHOOL DAYS, SCHOOL DAYS

Timeline:

I found the handwritten draft of this story. It was probably written around 1956. Virginia Rollins was 30 years old.

Real life reference:

This is a dark story, not sure of the genesis. At the time, my mother had been a teacher for approximately 9 years. Had she seen some cruelty to kids? She was a loving teacher, always looking out for the underdog.

*Five and Dime: Akin to current day "Dollar Store". There was actually a Five and Dime in Manhasset where we lived. Reference to "Five and Ten" store. "On 22 February 1879, Woolworth opened his **Great Five Cent Store** in Utica, New York, and it was his later success and expansion of that format as the F. W. Woolworth Company of that would create the American institution of the five and ten cent store, five and dime, or dime store." Wikipedia*

The sun had hardly set, and David had lied twice to his mother. Once when he said he had finished his homework so that she would allow him to go out into the damp evening air to dig worms out of the cold, hard ground. Secondly, about the worms. They weren't for Mr. Linehart's Science class as he had said. They were for Miss Hoswell. He couldn't tell his mother that. She wouldn't have believed it anyway. What would Miss Hoswell, eighth grade English teacher, want with worms? David grinned. He hated Miss Hoswell. The first day he had seen her behind the big desk in the eighth-grade room he had formed one opinion of her: fat. The second week he had found out two more things: he hated Miss Hoswell, and Miss Hoswell hated him.

From then on English class might as well have been Greek class. It began with assignments done sloppily; then David began to leave out parts of the exercises. Finally, he no longer bothered. It was no exertion to go to English class. Actually, English class came to him. He just stayed in the same seat he'd sat in since 8:30 in the morning. It was Mr. Linehart who packed up his books, his displays, rocks, and praying mantis and left the desk cleared for Miss Hoswell.

English class was the last class in the day. For almost twenty weeks he had watched Miss Hoswell come in, put down her books, move the dictionary to the left of the desk, the thesaurus to the right. More than twenty times he had seen Miss Hoswell return the dictionary to the right of the desk, the thesaurus to the left. Then he knew she was planning a lecture, preparatory to the scolding. That's when she was "mad."

Miss Hoswell thoroughly disliked boys, girls, and English in that order. She enjoyed disciplining. Her breath would come in short, little gasps and the color would mount from her collar to the edges of her wig-like red hair. During his short span in English class Miss Hoswell had sent him from the room nine times. In short, controlled gasps she had ridiculed him and herself.

"Get out! Get out, you little clown. You, you... insECT!"

And she had practically carried him and his collection of frogs, mice, turtles, and bugs to the door of the classroom each time. Then the novelty of animals and his going limp under her plump, short arms wore off and no longer brought the class to roars of laughter, only a few short snickers or a snort.

David turned to a new diversion. A born comic, he bought a false nose and a pair of spectacles from the Five and Dime. Lunch hours he entertained Sammy and his other friends with imitations of Miss Hoswell. It was no secret to the rest of the faculty that the eighth graders referred to the ample Miss Hoswell as "The Can."

One Monday, Miss Hoswell came upon the group in the playground. David was in the center twisting and squirming his little body into an imaginary corset and the rest were chanting:

"David's the man.
Hoswell's The Can!"

It was David who had to bear the brunt of her wrath. She kept him after school for two weeks straight. Took away his lunch hour, too. He refused to study his books while he stayed for her. She blamed it on his lack of brains.

"You'll work with those books, one way or another," she said, loading his arms with a dictionary, a geography textbook, a history book, and four or five other large volumes. "Stand up and hold those. Perhaps through the process of osmosis..."

David held the armload of books for over an hour every night of the two weeks after school. Many times, he wavered but he never gave in. He told no one. No one ever entered to see the slight, rather large-eared boy standing in the middle of the room with an armload of books.

Another time Miss Hoswell caught him looking out the window when he should have been writing a theme. She called his name sharply. A few minutes later she looked up. David was looking fully at her. She stared back. He didn't blink. Miss Hoswell fidgeted with the dictionary.

"Well, and what are <u>you</u> thinking about?"

David's answer came unexpectedly to both of them.

"You. You're fat. And sloppy."

This time Miss Hoswell went to his mother. His mother took away his privileges. No movies, no TV, no allowance. This was the first after-dinner privilege he'd had in a long time. This of going out and digging worms. And it wasn't exactly a privilege.

The next morning David left for school later than usual. He had to search for a small can put the worms in, something flat he could slide in his pocket. In the garbage pail where his mother put the cans she had opened and discarded he found a small sardine tin. The three fat worms fit just right after he had curled them carefully.

This was the day the Miss Hoswell had asked to have the eighth graders for the entire afternoon so that they could finish some grammar and the novel unit. That meant that English class would begin immediately after lunch. At twelve, rather than follow Sammy and the front row boys to the playground, David hung back.

"Miss Westberg, can I eat lunch in here today?" David asked.

"No," Miss Westberg said flatly, "it's not allowed."

"But I'm way behind in my novel unit. I've got to stay in to make up the work," pleaded David. "Please, Miss Westberg." His voice broke a little. "We're going to have to hand in all that stuff to Miss Hoswell this afternoon."

Miss Westberg had lifted her head from the paper and was watching him. David let his lower lip tremble. Miss Westberg looked quite taken in as she folded her paper.

"Well, I didn't know you were so conscientious, David."

He was pleased with himself. Maybe this year he would try out for the school play. He was really quite the actor.

Miss Westberg flashed a quick look at the clock. 12:10. She had already frittered away ten minutes of her precious lunch hour. Now she might not have time to finish her crossword puzzle.

"Oh, alright, but this time only." She snatched a lunch bag from a drawer in the desk, flicked a key locking the desk, and scurried to the door.

"But don't you dare let anyone else come into this room. In fact, I'll lock the door," which she did.

David was alone. He unwrapped his sandwich. Peanut butter and bacon. Milk, an apple. He finished it in seven minutes, according to the wall clock. He cleaned his desk. There was still lots of time before class began. He took out a piece of paper and began to do math problems. Soon the paper was covered with figures. He wadded the wax paper his sandwich had been in and shot for the basket. Perfect shot. The apple core missed and skidded under the desk. David left it there. He walked towards the desk. On the way, he dropped the math paper in the basket.

He reached into the inner pocket of his jacket. His mother had made him wear a good suit and shirt because they were going to his Aunt's house for dinner that night. She lived far out, and they'd have to leave early. They could save time by his being all dressed. His eyes examined the desk. He tried the drawers. They were locked. Where could he put the worms? The blotter was too obvious. She always touched the dictionary. No. Too obvious, too. But he had three worms. David leaned towards the blackboard while he thought. He felt the chalk tray in his back. The chalk tray. She always wrote the next day's exercise first thing. It would be perfect.

David opened the tin. The worms had not moved. He

dumped two out into the chalk tray. They began to crawl. David picked them up one by one and rubbed them in the chalk dust until they were white. They looked like slender, curved pieces of chalk. David staggered the worms about one foot apart from each other. Then he timed them. Four times. It took the furthest one two minutes to reach the spot where Miss Hoswell usually kept her chalk. It would be perfect.

At 12:55 the class ambled in. David stayed by the chalk tray. Exactly as the last bell rang Miss Hoswell walked in. David stopped at two different spots at the tray. Then he sat down.

Miss Hoswell stared the class into silence. She turned to the board and reached for the chalk. The worm had arrived on time. There was perfect contact and then Miss Hoswell's scream. Her fingers seemed reluctant to let the worm go even though she shook her arm furiously. Finally, the white, chalk-like object fell to the floor.

Out of a white face, Miss Hoswell's eyes challenged the class. David felt a desire to laugh and run. He was frightened and exuberant. She was really mad. If she knew who. Suddenly he felt a tightening in his stomach. The tin was on his desk! He had forgotten to throw the tin away. The third worm was coming to life. It seemed years before he dared look up. It was too late. Her first suspect, Miss Hoswell had directed her challenge to David, and she had also seen the tin. She shivered over him.

"Get in that closet... get in!" Her last words ended in a shriek. It was against school rules to put anyone in a closet. She was too angry to care. David had to make a show of nonchalance. He stopped at the desk, stopped down to pick up the worm. It was striped now where some of the chalk dust had rubbed off. He flicked it in the basket. It rested on the paper covered with figures.

The supply closet was small and crowded with books, the shelves crowded with books. The floor was littered with rubbers and shoes. Right in the center on the ceiling there was a big hook.

A coat hung from it. Miss Hoswell snatched it down and pushed David into the chair directly under the hook.

"Sit there!"

From her seat at the desk Miss Hoswell could only see the open door. David could look out over the whole class. He waved, put his thumb to his nose, slumped in the chair. With each movement the front row boys snickered, cautiously at first.

David examined the closet with exaggerated interest. The floor, the shelves, the ceiling. Quietly and carefully he stood on the chair. Miss Hoswell read on, engrossed. She wasn't one of those readers who look up every three or four words. She didn't even look up when she turned the page.

David bowed again in Miss Hoswell's direction, tongue out. He reached for the hook. His feet swung free of the chair, touching shelves, books, the walls. With a graceful swing, David chinned himself on the hook... once, twice, three times. The front row boys forgot themselves and giggled out loud. Miss Hoswell's chins trembled. She walked wordlessly to the closet door. David had returned to the chair. He looked innocently at his teacher.

She reached for the door. "You little clown. See how you like entertaining yourself for a little while."

She shut the door, but not completely. It was ajar just a crack, enough for David to look out and see across three rows of seats. They could see only movement behind the slight opening. David sat in the half-gloom. He giggled nervously aloud. The boys had heard him. They giggled encouragement. Miss Hoswell read. David stood on the chair. He swung himself again. His foot knocked the shelf, loudly. This time so the boys would know what he was doing. He thumped against the wall with one foot, with both feet. He heard the laughter. Miss Hoswell's voice slowed somewhat. He rested on the chair a minute. He was warm. His jacket hindered his movements. He took it off, threw it on the floor. He ran his fingers under his tight collar and then unbuttoned the collar and loosened the tie so that there was about an inch between the collar and tie. Then he swung again. He thumped the door. It flew open.

They had never seen Miss Hoswell walk so fast before. In what seemed one motion she reached for the door and slammed it shut. Tight.

He felt as if all the walls were closing in. He wanted to kick open the door. He remembered his room at night when he first put out the light. It was dark at first but if he shut his eyes real tight for a minute or so, the black of the room wouldn't appear as dark as the black of the closed eyes. He did it now. Things began to feel better. He felt for objects. His fingers touched shoes, books, shelves. He stood up on the chair and reached for the hook. He'd show her. He grasped firmly and began to swing furiously, thumping angrily against the shelves, the door, the walls. The noise was alarmingly loud.

Suddenly David felt the hook turning under his hand. He swung again. He was revolving. The hook went around and around. He propelled the hook faster, swinging his legs harder and twisting his body, each time thumping the door. It was a wild thrill, suspended in a closed closet in the dark. David pretended he was above tall buildings. It was nighttime. The crowd below was looking up, waiting. David swung by one hand, waving with the other. Then both hands. He chinned himself. His feet touched the chair. This was to be the defiant act that thrilled the crowd. He pushed hard on the chair, twisting his body so as to revolve and at the same time exerting strength to chin himself as he revolved. He pushed too hard. His feet pushed the chair over. He revolved a couple of times, his tie caught in the hook. The boys outside heard the noise and snickered. Inside, David tried to raise himself higher. His air was cut off. His feet reached for the chair, so mockingly near but he couldn't find it. Desperate, he thumped the walls.

Miss Hoswell read on. The thumping had stopped completely. The sun had reached farther into the room and wrapped around the legs of the chairs and high socks of the girls. At first the silence had been more deafening that the thumping but the novelty of the swinging boy in the closet had mellowed under the influence of the droning voice coming from behind the book held at arm's length on the desk. Now and then eyes would be directed to the closet door but did not linger there. The stares traveled upwards to the clock above the closed door. Five minutes for the final bell. Four. Two. The bell. Miss Hoswell's book snapped shut before the first eager boy was out of his seat. Sammy lingered behind.

"Wait for David outside, Samuel. He'll be quite a while."

Sammy moved slowly past the wastebasket. The worm was half-covered by a piece of scratch paper. There were numbers all over the paper. He passed the closet door.

Miss Hoswell cleared off her desk. She moved the dictionary to the left side of her desk, the thesaurus to the right. The board needed erasing. She lowered the shades. Miss Hoswell had mentally prepared her lecture. She was ready to open the door now. She walked to the desk, moved the thesaurus to the left of the desk, the dictionary to the right.

With one hand on her hip she turned the knob.

"Come out, David."

She had not looked in. There was no response. The silence irritated her. She turned. It was dark in the closet. Dark and quiet. But not too dark to see an overturned chair. And over the chair, not touching anything, legs. Legs in dark trousers. Before the greatest blackness came, Miss Hoswell saw a little boy, suspended, swinging from a hook, held there by a tie which seemed to have four knots.

He was quite quiet, now.

ALBERT, THE ALLEY-CAT WHO MADE GOOD

Timeline:

This was probably written around 1968. Virginia Rollins was 42.

Real life reference:

We had just moved to a house that had an alley behind it and my sister Patty had just gotten her first cat, Tinkerbell.

One day Albert walked across a box of Jamie's finger paints. He tracked back and forth across some big squares of clean white paper.

"Look at what Albert painted!" Jamie exclaimed to his mother.

His mother showed the squares of white covered with pinky-green and purply-orange cat tracks to Jamie's art teacher.

"See the wonderful work Jamie's cat, Albert, can do," she said.

"AMAZING!" said the art teacher.

"LOOK at this example of cat-art," the art teacher told an artist friend.

The artist friend took it to a bigger artist who owned a gallery.

"How original," said the big artist. He hung the squares on easels in his gallery and sent out 700 invitations:

YOU ARE INVITED TO
THE WORLD PREMIERE
OF A NEW ART FORM:
CAT-ART

Everyone came in big, long cars. The women wore shiny dresses and pearl necklaces. The men wore little bow ties and pants with satin stripes. Albert sat on a high-back chair and Jamie and his mother stood next to him. Jamie patted Albert's head and said, "Don't be frightened, Albert."

But Albert wasn't one bit frightened. He liked all the attention.

The men peered at Albert's paintings through tiny half glasses. The women peered through little glasses that looked like plastic lollipops on the end of a long pink straw.

"Masterful!" said a man with a beard.

"A work of art!" said a lady who knew all about art.

"Um-HUH," said a third who knew what she liked.

Albert's photograph was in all the papers. He was on three television shows. At a party full of important people, he drank sparkling milk from a girl's glass slipper.

One day the big artist came to Jamie's house.
"Albert is very famous now," he said.

"Oh, yes," said Jamie proudly. "Everyone comes to see him. He pointed to a big pile of presents in the warm red box. "And everyone brings him lots of presents."

There was a solid goldfish for Albert to nibble on, a silver bell to jingle on, a white furry ball to pounce on.

"Very nice," said the big artist. "But Albert must come to live with me now."

"Oh, no." Jamie hugged Albert. "Albert wouldn't leave me."

"I can teach him many things," said the big artist. He held out an emerald green catnip. Albert swallowed it greedily.

"He needs me," said Jamie, picking up Albert. The big artist took a tiny tuna tidbit from his vest pocket and dangled it.

"He needs ME," he said. Albert jumped from Jamie's arms and rubbed against the big artist's legs. He eyed the tiny tuna tidbit and purred a song of "take-me-with-you."

So, Albert left the little house Jamie had made for him. He went to live with the big artist in a huge room filled with fancy furniture. There was a red velvet carpet on the floor and two silk pillows, one gold and one the color of cherry blossoms.

Every day he painted a new picture. The big artist gave him an "O" at the end of his name. Now, when the big artist sent out invitations, they said:

PAINTINGS BY ALBERTO

Jamie tried to be glad for his old-time friend. Very often, though, he stood in front of the warm red box that was empty now and sighed, "I wish Albert had never become an artist."

Once Jamie saw his old friend in a magazine picture. He was romping through a field of buttercups. Once he saw him riding down the Avenue in a yellow car. Jamie waved out but Alberto ignored him. Maybe he couldn't see him because the sun was in his eyes. One blustery Sunday in March Jamie saw a picture in the newspaper of a cat artist and his paintings.

"Look!" he said, showing the picture to his mother. "Another cat artist. His name is Gilbert."

Jamie turned the picture this way and that way.

"Of course," he said. "He's not as good as Albert." Jamie was very loyal.

The next day, two more new cat artists appeared on a television show. One was a blue-eyed Siamese cat who painted with his tail, great big swishes, and swashes of blue and lavender. Pretty soon there were so many cat artists painting that all the store windows up and down the avenue were filled with cat art. Some were not as good as Albert's. Some were better.

The big artist hung a large sign in his window.

PAINTINGS BY ALBERTO, THE FIRST CAT ARTIST

But when people came inside the gallery they walked right by Alberto. A very rich lady waved aside Alberto's paintings with a hand covered with rings. "I don't want those. Those are too common!" She looked down her nose at Alberto. "Unless he can do something... different!"

"Like my portrait," said her daughter who had a very long nose.

"Or flowers and fruit," snapped her father, tapping his cane on the red velvet carpet.

They all pointed at Alberto. "CAN he?"

Alberto stretched his legs and cat-cleaned a paw. He sniffed at some tiny tuna tidbits.

"Alberto!" The big artist pointed to a clean, white square of paper and a box of paints.

"Paint!" he said. He took the dish of tiny tunas away. Alberto turned his head from side to side. He yawned. Slowly, he strolled across the clean white paper.

"A-ha! You'll see!" The big artist rubbed his hands and smiled at the very rich lady. The rich lady smiled at her daughter. The daughter smiled at the father. The father tapped his cane and said, "A-ha! Let's see."

Alberto covered the clean white square with pinky-green and purply-orange cat tracks.

"You call that DIFFERENT!" snapped the rich lady.

"You call that ORIGINAL!" sniffed the daughter.

"You call him an ARTIST!" snorted the father.

They swept past Alberto through the door. They almost knocked down Jamie, who had been peeking through.

"Out, out, OUT!" shouted the big artist, slamming the door in Jamie's face. Jamie hid against the wall and peeked through the window. The big artist towered over Alberto.

"Imposter! You are no artist!" He tore Alberto's paintings off the easels and tied them in big squares to send to a wallpaper factory.

"Ungrateful, lazy cat!"
He took away the two silk pillows.

"You... alley-cat!"

He took away the high-back chair.

"Go downstairs and chase mice, ALBERT!"

He took the "O" away from Alberto. He threw Albert down the cellar stairs and forgot all about him.

"Albert. Albert." Jamie called and called. He tried to open the door, but the door was locked. It began to get dark and Jamie went home.

That night Albert slipped through a window in the back of the store. He crept along the edge of the moonlight, then he disappeared in the shadows of the alley. He was just an alley-cat again.

Jamie found him there one April afternoon. He was covered with April rain.

"Poor Albert," said Jamie, picking him up. He put the muddy wet bundle of fur in his jacket.

"You need a bath," he scolded.

"You need some milk," he cried.

"You need ME." And Jamie took him home again.

Albert crawled into the warm red box with the yellow-flowered pillow. Jamie gave him all his friendship and Albert gave <u>him</u> all his love.

PETER'S PENNY MAGIC

Timeline:

Probably written before 1968 as it had Webster Ave. as the address. Virginia Rollins was approximately 42 years old.

Real life reference:

I can remember my mom counting out the pennies onto the dining room table when I was just a child.

She had also written a poem called My Penny Jar which was published for $3.00 on Oct 4, 1965 which was also about 127 pennies and similar to this story.

C arefully Peter tucked a brown paper bag into his desk. He could hardly wait for school to begin.

"Hey, Peter," called Ralph. "Let's see what you brought for Show & Tell today."

Peter shook his head.

"Not now," he said. "It's a surprise."

It was very important to Peter that everyone liked his surprise. This was a new school for him and his very first week in it. He wanted to be good friends with all the boys and girls in the class.

"It doesn't look very big," said Ralph. "Look at what I

brought." He flew a huge silver-colored airplane around Peter's head.

"Watch the wheels," he cried. "I can make them disappear." Two little doors seemed to open mysteriously to swallow up the wheels.

"Like magic," said Betty, who was watching.

"My surprise is like magic, too," said Peter.

"Really, Peter?" asked Betty eagerly.

"I can make what I have change into something else," said Peter.

"That's not so much," said Ralph, zooming his plane into a crash dive. "I've seen that kind of magic before."

"Besides," chimed in Ralph's friend Chuck, "you can't do anything with an old magic trick after you finish, like play with it or anything."

"Well, I can with this," said Peter. "Besides, in the end it changes into a big red wagon."

"THIS we have to see," said Ralph, rolling his eyes.

After Miss Richards finished the spelling words for the day, the class quickly formed a circle for Show & Tell. First Ralph showed the class his shiny, silver plane with the disappearing wheels. Betty showed a beautiful piece of cloth that her father had brought back from a trip to India. It was decorated with gold and silver thread and Betty said it was all made by hand. Albert had a piece of lava that came from a real volcano in Hawaii. He passed it around and everyone felt the bubbly, bumpy shape.

Betty raised her hand.

"Please, Miss Richards," she said. "Peter says he has a magic surprise. Could he be next?"

"Of course," said Miss Richards. "Magic is exciting."

Peter reached inside his desk and carefully pulled out the brown paper bag. He put his hand in the bag and said, "THIS is my surprise!"

Proudly he held up a small jar. Everyone looked.

"That's just a jar filled with pennies," said Ralph.

"I thought you said you could change what you had into something else," said a disappointed Betty.

"I can," said Peter. "See." He counted out five pennies. "I could change these five pennies into a nickel. Or I can take ten pennies and change them into a dime. I could take twenty-five and change them into a quarter."

"How many pennies would Peter need to change them into a one-dollar bill?" asked Miss Richards.

Ralph's arm shot up. "I know that. One hundred. But I bet he doesn't have one hundred pennies."

"Oh, yes I do," answered Peter. "I have one hundred twenty-seven in this penny jar."

"Wow," said Ralph. "That's a dollar and twenty-seven cents!" He was impressed.

"You said you could play with it and that in the end it would change into a red wagon. Let's see you change it into a red wagon," demanded Chuck.

"I'll show you how I play with them in a minute," said Peter, grinning, "but I have to wait a while before I can change it into a red wagon. When I get 395 of these pennies, I'm going to take them down to Brighton's Hardware Store and buy the big red wagon they have in the window. It costs $8.95 but my dad said he'd pay the last five dollars."

Everyone laughed. Peter stepped to the teacher's desk.

"I'll show you how I play with them," he said. "You can do lots of things with pennies."

He began to put the pennies into rows. "I can pretend they are soldiers. Look. Twelve rows of marching soldiers, ten in each row.

"One hundred and twenty soldiers," called Ralph quickly. "And seven left over."

"Right." Peter scooped up the pennies and began to pile them very high. I can stack them like this in two piles. Each pile is fifty-three pennies high. I have twenty-one left."

"Or," he said, moving the pennies to form letters, "I can take exactly sixty-four and spell my sister Nancy's name."

"You could wind them like a big copper snake along the floor," suggested Betty.

"You could slide them flat or roll them on their edges," said Chuck.

"Hey, Pete. Let me try. Let me try," everyone began to clamor.

The big silver plane with the disappearing wheels sat unnoticed on a chair. The shiny cloth from India was folded neatly on the teacher's desk. The piece of lava rested on the chalk tray. The whole class was in a circle around Peter and his penny jar.

Peter smiled. He <u>knew</u> they would like his penny magic.

PUMPKINS IS
FOR EATIN'

Timeline:

Mom had handwritten her address, again, 68 Webster Ave., on the yellowed pages of this story with many scribbled changes throughout. Again, must have been before 1968. Virginia Rollins was 42 years old.

Real life reference:

There used to be a Five and Dime on Plandome Road in Manhasset that I used to save up my change and go to, happy to buy a trinket or two with just a few coins.

The young characters were similar in age to my brother and me at that time.

The reference to "Mama" is what my mom called her mother.

Signs of the times:

Raggedy Ann Doll; "The exact details of the origins of the Raggedy Ann doll and related stories, which were created by Johnny Gruelle, are not specifically known, although numerous myths and legends about the doll's origins have been widely repeated. As Gruelle's wife, Myrtle, reported, it was her husband who retrieved a long-forgotten, homemade rag doll from the attic of his parents' Indianapolis home sometime around the turn of the twentieth century before the couple's daughter was born. Although the incident is unconfirmed, Myrtle Gruelle recalled, "There was something he wanted from the attic. While he was rummaging around for it, he found an old rag doll his mother had made for his sister. He said then that the doll would make a good story." Wikipedia

<u>Related vernacular:</u>

"Where the dickens": "Let's focus in on dickens as the important word here, since there are lots of different expressions with it in, such as what the dickens, where the dickens, the dickens you are!, and the dickens you say! It goes back a lot further than Charles Dickens, though it does seem to have been borrowed from the English surname, most likely sometime in the sixteenth century or before. (The surname itself probably derives from Dickin or Dickon, familiar diminutive forms of Dick.) It was — and still is, though people hardly know it anymore — a euphemism for the Devil." Worldwidewords.org

"Nose to the grindstone": "Meaning "to work hard or focus heavily on work." If he'd keep his nose to the grindstone a bit more, he could be a pretty good student." Wiktionary

Martha sat back on her heels and rubbed her back with a moan. She looked around for her brother, Jeff, and saw him coming towards her with the big wheelbarrow almost filled with pumpkins. That would mean it was time to quit. Martha fell back on her hands and knees and tugged at the big pumpkin she had just loosened from the vine. Her dark hair fell over her eyes as she wiggled the pumpkin along the ground.

Jeff called her. "Come on! I'm beat and I'm cold."

She too felt no warmth from the late October afternoon sun which seemed to be wrapping up the world in a golden glow.

"We've been here all afternoon. There aren't any more pumpkins anyhow," he added as he easily picked up the heavy one with which she had been struggling.

"Give it to me, flyweight," he mocked, and he dumped it on top of the rest of the pumpkins in the wheelbarrow. He stood at least two heads taller than his eight-year-old sister. Martha's nose wrinkled and she flicked a quick blow off her brother's arm.

They started slowly down the long row to the dirt path that led out of the pumpkin field, Jeff, and Martha each holding onto one of the wheelbarrow's handles. Martha walked clumsily beside Jeff trying to fit all of them on the same path.

"All these pumpkins," she said angrily. "You'd think there'd be enough to keep some for ourselves. Even just one."

Two of the largest pumpkins on the top rolled off the wheelbarrow and hit the ground.

"Martha be careful," warned Jeff. "Uncle Caleb will kill you if you break one of those or crack 'em. Don't complicate things, you know the guys are coming over to pick me up for a game of touch football later and I've still got chores to do."

Even though it wouldn't be dark for a while yet everything all around already darkened for Martha at Jeff's words.

"Most likely Uncle Caleb will find something extra for us to do -- even if he has to think very hard about it."

She wondered why Uncle Caleb always seemed to spoil their fun. It had always been hard for the two of them to understand Uncle Caleb even though he was their father's brother. He seemed almost like a stranger in his brusque, hard-working manner. Their father had been quiet and soft-spoken. He had always had time to share a few minutes with them to fix a bike or hold a shaky ladder so they could climb to the top of a tempting tree. He had taught them to make bird houses for the birds who had been sort of friends to them in the loneliness of a farm on the outskirts of town. Then three years ago when he died and Uncle Caleb came to live with them, all that had changed.

Like these pumpkins. Martha knew that Jeff didn't care. He'd grown out of witches and costumes and pumpkin faces, but she hadn't. All the kids her size walked around trick or treating holding candle-lit orange faces in their hands.

Last year when Ma had decided that Martha would be old enough to carry her own without worrying about putting herself on fire, Uncle Caleb had said, "Wouldn't waste a pumpkin on such nonsense."

This year when he caught Martha sizing them, he grunted again. "All good for sellin' this year. All good."

"You mean I can't have a pumpkin to cut out or carry or anything?" cried Martha. "Not even a little one?"

"Nope," answered Uncle Caleb.

Now as they approached the barn Uncle Caleb came towards them. He buttoned his heavy knit sweater around his neck and slapped his hands together. "Getting' cold, kids. Go up home and get on some jackets over those sweaters." He took the wheelbarrow from Jeff and wheeled it to the old car that stood in the driveway in front of the barn. His voice and ways were gruff, but he was very gentle as he transferred two of the roundest, most perfect pumpkins to the car. Martha stood watching.

"I'll take these to Rev. Parker's missus myself," Uncle Caleb said. "Jeff, I told you and Martha to go on up to the house for jackets."

"I was hoping I could just run up to Baker's Field on my bike to see if the guys are having a game."

" No!" snapped Uncle Caleb as he slid in behind the wheel. "No game tonight. You and your sister go down to the stand and take those pumpkins with you. Stayin' open late tonight. Sold out just about all we have 'cept for them. Sure to be lots of folks late shoppin'. Tomorrow's Halloween Eve, ya know." He turned on the key and the motor sputtered.

"Uncle Caleb," shouted Martha as the car moved slowly forward. "Uncle Caleb. Wait!"

The motor sputtered, then stopped. "Don't stop me once I 'm goin'!" yelled Uncle Caleb. "Fool thing to do. What do you want?"

"Please, Uncle Caleb, please couldn't I have even just one little pumpkin for tomorrow night? Please?"

Uncle Caleb's pipe bounced up and down in his mouth as he bit out the words. "Nope! Pumpkins is for eatin'!"

"But nobody, nobody who buys them from you eats them," argued Martha. Her eyes were filling with tears and her voice was loud.

"Fools then," he muttered angrily as he forced the car to start. It jerked out of the driveway.

Martha's cold hands were still extended in a gesture of pleading as the car chugged from sight. She was trying not to sob, and she was breathing in jerks as the car had done when it began to warm up. Jeff kicked a stone and it skipped across the driveway sending bursts of gravel flying. "Come on, Pee Wee," he said. He made a half-move to comfort her in some way then changing his mind jabbed her on the elbow as he ran ahead.

"Race you to the stands!"

Jeff had been waiting for some time when Martha finally came. She had been crying.

"Aw, Martha," he tried to console her. "Don't feel so bad. Maybe I can get you one of those fake pumpkins at the 5 and 10 and you can carry that. O.K.?"

Martha's eyes came to life. "Do you really think so Jeff?" Then her shoulders dropped again. "But how will you get to town to buy it and anyhow, even if you could get there, where would you get the money?"

"Oh, I got it. I'll use my special money," Jeff said in a breezy way.

"Your special money," echoed. Martha. "Oh, Jeff, you can't. That's what Mama gives you. She wouldn't like it. You can't do that."

Every week Jeff's mother took a small bit from the already small income of the eggs and gave it to Jeff towards buying something he had wanted for nearly two years. A new football, a good leather one so he could practice kicking right in the yard and fields.

"Anyhow Jeff, you've been saving a long time and it'll be baseball time before you can save enough again."

"Aw, what's fifty cents?" asked Jeff gruffly but when Martha looked at him, she knew how much fifty cents would mean.

And yet, Halloween Eve was almost there and when all the kids came, she'd be the only one without a pumpkin and everybody would laugh and say it was because Uncle Caleb was so tight and mean. And he was! He was! she thought vehemently. She swallowed hard and forgot about Jeff's football and said, "Thanks Jeff. Thanks a million!"

Jeff circled round and round the stand with his bike once in a while sliding out into the road.

"Uncle Caleb put this stand too close to the road," shouted Jeff as his tire bumped a pumpkin and sent his bike skidding into the street. "Should be back a bit."

"Well, he wanted to be sure the cars saw us before they were already past us," answered Martha. She was humming. Tomorrow night could come now; she'd be ready. Carefully she placed the little coin box on the inside shelf of the stand. Then she arranged three pumpkins on the countertop: small, big, bigger. She pushed the sign farther out.

"Pumpkins Here. All Sizes." The sign read. No one stopped by. More and more cars were beginning to whir by.

Suddenly Martha had an idea. "Jeff, Jeff," she called.

Jeff didn't look up from where he was slowly revolving the wheel of his bike and carefully checking the tire for any leaks.

Martha ran from the stand to him. Her hand on his shoulder, she cried, "Jeff, look. No one's coming. I can handle the stand for a while. Why don't you go up to the field and play some football? Uncle Caleb won't be back before dark. You'll be back by then."

Jeff shook his head. "Nah. Can't. Uncle Caleb would kill me."

"He wouldn't even know."

Jeff stood up and wiped his hands on his blue jeans.

"Go ahead, Jeff, so the guys won't think it's just 'cause you don't want to play."

"Huh!" snorted Jeff. "I want to play all right!" Still he remembered what Archie Rogers had commented last week when he heard that Jeff couldn't play that maybe they oughta get a new halfback...someone they could count on.

Well, he was the best around. They ought to remember that. Jeff spoke in a more than half convinced voice. "Maybe you're right. Listen Martha. I won't play. I'll just up and tell 'em why I can't play tonight and then I'll come right back. O.K.?"

"Sure, Jeff," said Martha. "Only come back before dark."

Jeff sped out to the street on his bike. "Maybe I'll just go through one play," he called back laughing as she waved goodbye.

Martha waved back then settled back on a stool in the stand and waited. Time seemed to go so slowly in the stand. She amused herself by guessing car colors but soon tired of that. Stepping outside the stand, she leaned against it. Across the street the sun pointed long fingers of light on the swampy fields. It seemed to spotlight what appeared to be cattails and lots of milk weeds. Wouldn't they make a nice surprise for her mother? Martha looked back at the stand. She could see anyone who came easily enough. All she'd have to do would be to run back across the street to take care of any customers.

Martha hadn't noticed from the stand that there were so many beautiful colored leaves too. The plants and leaves were becoming a sizable bunch on the ground where she piled them. The cars were passing more often, and they were going faster. Getting near dinner time, she guessed. Jeff should be getting back soon.

Martha was reaching for an extra special golden-red leaf when she heard the screeching of brakes. She turned quickly in time to see a big, black car coming towards the stand. It was traveling too fast to make the curve. It swerved back and forth trying to get back on the other side of the road. It was too dark to see the driver. It swerved too far. The car streaked off the road for a split second. Martha raised her hands to her face and screamed along with the brakes.

There was a sickening sound of splintering wood, some thuds, and brakes screeching. Then the car was back on the road, streaking forward on its way again. It never stopped. Martha stood rooted to the spot. She couldn't move. Across the street a broken jumble of a half-knocked down stand loomed at her. And all around, pumpkins ---pumpkins in the street, on the ground, broken, cracked, oozing orange. Martha stared at a pumpkin that teetered on the edge of the road. The sound of a car with a half familiar whir to it came. The pumpkin would be crushed if it went under the wheels. But the wheels never reached the pumpkin.

They turned and drove into the drive, in front of what used to be the stand. Martha felt like she was going to be sick. It was Uncle Caleb.

Uncle Caleb jumped from his car so fast that he left the motor running. He ran from pumpkin to pumpkin waving his arms, trying to straighten up the tumbled down stand as if it were made of children's blocks that only had to be stacked again. Martha couldn't hear what he was saying but the look on his face was enough. She didn't need to hear.

Suddenly as if he remembered there was something else in the world besides pumpkins and stands, he thundered, "Martha! Jeff! **Where the dickens** are you?"

Martha crossed the street. The sound his voice had already started her crying. Uncle Caleb was hammering words at her.

"Where were you? What do you mean leaving the stand alone? Who did this?" He never waited for an answer. Instead he picked up one of the boards that had been on the side of the stand. "Where is Jeff?" he roared.

"J-J-Jeff," Martha would never tell him where Jeff was. She didn't have to. Down the road came Jeff. He was pedaling fast with his head down aware of the late hour and he was almost on top of them before he saw anything. When he did, his face went white.

"Martha," his voice shook with concern, "Martha, what happened to you?"

"Never mind!" screamed Uncle Caleb. "Now, what happened you say! What do you mean riding off on that bike?"

He was waving the board closer and closer to Jeff.

"I-I—I went to the field...," began Jeff.

The color of Uncle Caleb's face was the purple blue color of the fall grapes. He couldn't speak any longer. Martha feared for Jeff.

"I told him to go!" she found her tongue. "It wasn't any-body's fault. A car couldn't make the curve and hit the stand. Jeff said before that that the stand was too close to the road. That's all. That's all."

Grabbing Martha Uncle Caleb spun her around and shook her so hard that her head bobbed like the head on her oldest **Rag-gedy Ann doll**.

"That's all? That's all?" His voice was unbelieving. "Look at the waste. The waste. What about the money we could've used from these?" He pushed her from him.

Uncle Caleb was breathing hard when he turned to Jeff. But something in Jeff's look stopped his words. The boy seemed to be taller---almost as tall as himself---as he stood stone faced before him. His words that cut through the silence were colder than the October night that was closing in around them.

"It wasn't Martha's fault. It's not fair to blame her." The boy's voice passed judgement on the man standing before him in the debris of the pumpkin stand. "You---you didn't even care what happened to her. You didn't even say 'Thank God she wasn't in the stand when it happened."

He turned to walk away shouting over his shoulder. "All you cared about was your pumpkins. Your rotten pumpkins!"

Uncle Caleb stood a long time without moving, staring at the still shouldered shadow walking away in the dusk.

Martha and Jeff sat quietly at the table as their mother filled their plates. Uncle Caleb wasn't there for dinner. She wasn't anxious for the children now as she had been when it started to get dark and Martha had come stumbling in crying. She was quiet while Jeff told her in a shaky voice what had happened. She bit her lip when he came to his words with Uncle Caleb.

As she passed them their plates of thick, hot soup, she said, "Uncle Caleb is a---a different sort of man from your father. He does the best he can." She buttered a hot roll for Martha but forgot to hand it to her. "Your father, well, you father did the best he could too. But I guess he wasn't too practical a man. Things here on the farm were sort of, well, messed up when Dad died." It hurt her to say that about their father. They could tell. Jeff took a quick gulp of milk and Martha bent her head lower over the soup.

Mother went on. "The truth is, children, that without Uncle Caleb and his way of doing things---we, we'd be pretty bad off. We couldn't have gotten along without him."

She walked to the kitchen window and peered into the dark. Nothing moved outside. Uncle Caleb had come home from the stand without a word. He had come into the kitchen, put on a jacket, and had driven away in the old car. He had been gone a long time. Jeff and Martha hated the silence around them. Their spoons struck hard on the sides of the bowls and they could hear each other swallow.

After dinner Jeff and Martha went out to the barn to finish their chores. Usually Jeff went alone, and Martha helped Mother in the kitchen but tonight Mother had urged them to go together. Martha rolled the wheelbarrow out to the tool shed and Jeff was about to latch the door when the headlights of a car lit up the dark.

"Jeff. It's Uncle Caleb," whispered Martha. Jeff didn't answer. He turned his back to the lights and walked toward the barn.

"C'mon Mar," he said. "We've gotta take care of the cow."

Uncle Caleb hardly ever went into the house through the front door but tonight he did. When the children came in through the back door, he was nowhere to be seen.

"To bed, Martha," said her mother looking up from her sewing. Her fingers touched Martha's face gently as she said, "Martha, your Uncle Caleb is in his room. I want you to speak to him." Martha's eyes questioned. "Say good-night to him," said Mother in answer to them.

Martha looked to Jeff. "And Jeff," added Mother biting off a piece of thread matter-of-factly, "when Martha goes to bed, you are to go to Uncle Caleb's room." Jeff's shoulder stiffened and he stopped turning the page of the magazine he was looking through. She continued, "You are to apologize. Caleb is your uncle, your guardian." She didn't say anymore. She knew Jeff would do what she asked.

Martha climbed the stairs slowly. She wished she could go up one stair and back down two so she would take a long, long time getting there. In the hall a light showed under Uncle Caleb's door. With a big breath Martha raised her hand and knocked. No answer. She knocked again.

"Uncle Caleb?" Her voice seemed small even to herself. "Uncle Caleb, it's Martha. May I come in?"

"No. Don't come in." The answer that shot out to her in the dimness of the hall shocked Martha so that she jumped a little. "Go to bed," it said.

The cold feeling in the bottom of Martha's stomach didn't go away even when she had snuggled under the blankets in her long, flannel gown. Her hands that pulled the blankets closer around her were like ice. Only her eyes were burning hot from the tears that were trying to push their way out and she wouldn't let them.

Everything was all jumbled up and confused in her mind. Nothing seemed clear. It was like her room in the dark. She knew where everything was and should be but in the dark even the chairs and dresser seemed to take on different shapes. Uncle Caleb was good to them. Except for today when he had been so upset. Uncle Caleb had never laid a hand on her or Jeff. And he had come far away from his own home to be with them. He had shrugged it off saying he was a bachelor and it didn't matter where "a bachelor hung his hat."

"It isn't easy being with children when you're not used to having them around," Mother had said to Uncle Caleb when he had been there the first day.

"No matter. They're people," Uncle Caleb had answered. "Just like everyone else."

Martha began to feel warm deep down inside. His hard work and hard words had been to keep the family together. Why they might had had to break up the family, separate, if it hadn't been for Uncle Caleb. Her hold on the blankets loosened and her lips moved as she began to think out loud to herself. "He took on all of us. We only had to take on him." Her head began to feel heavy from all the thoughts rushing around as she began to realize that it had been much harder for Uncle Caleb than it had been for her and Jeff.

The sound of her name being called awakened her. All sorts of busy little dreams had crowded her sleep and made her feel that she hadn't been sleeping at all.

"Martha." In the doorway stood Uncle Caleb. The sound of his voice made her feel like someone had opened a window and just a breath of cold air had shot in. "I want you to get up," he said, "and come to my room."

Martha rubbed her eyes. He was gone. Had he been there or was this something she was dreaming? Quickly she slipped from under the warm blankets and stepped into the cold of the hall. The door to Uncle Caleb's room was open and she heard voices coming from the room. There were Uncle Caleb's and---Jeff's. Her heartbeat fast. It was no dream. Uncle Caleb wanted her to come to his room.

The sudden brightness of the lights burning in the room hurt her eyes that had grown accustomed to the dark. She put her hands to her eyes as if to screen out something she didn't want to see. Uncle Caleb was sitting in the rocking chair, his pipe in his mouth. Jeff was standing hands behind his back in front of the small table that held Uncle Caleb's magazines and pipe tobacco. Her mother sat next to the table. Jeff blocked most of the table, but Martha could see that it was covered with newspapers that draped over the side.

"Step aside a bit, Jeff," said Uncle Caleb. As Jeff moved a bit to the side, Martha saw that in his hand he held a knife, a jack knife. Martha's heart sank. Uncle Caleb's. She shot a quick glance at Uncle Caleb to see what he would do, what he would say. Instead, he took a puff on his pipe and then waved it at Jeff saying, "Move all the way, Jeff. Guess she can't see."

Jeff moved away from the table. There in the center stood a round pumpkin, just the perfect size for carving. A lid had been cut off. On the table was a little mound of the insides that had been scooped out. Jeff was looking at her with a wide grin on his face. Her mother was smiling, too.

Martha was really confused. Uncle Caleb got up slowly from the rocker and came to her with an arm outstretched.

"In case you don't recognize it, it's one of Mrs. Parker's."

Martha shook her head. "Didn't she want it?"

"No. Guess she thought this was a better use for it." He took her hand and held it tight in his. "It's for you, Martha, for tomorrow night. Jeff is goin' to make the face for you."

Jeff began to cut the eye of the face.

Uncle Caleb said watching him, "See. Uses that knife real fine. Fact is, I may be giving it to him to keep real soon."

Uncle Caleb looked down at the small nightgowned figure standing next to him. She wasn't saying anything.

"Don't you want the pumpkin, Martha?" he asked uneasily.

"Oh, yes," replied Martha very quickly. "But you always said...."

"Pumpkins is for eatin'. That's what I always said. "I know, I know." He pointed his pipe at her and said, "Foolishness. Just like puttin' your **nose so close to the grindstone**, you can't see what you're working' on." His arm tightened around her and he said in a very quiet voice. "Just like I always said, kids were people, just like everybody else. Well," he looked at Jeff, "a pretty grown-up person showed me that kids are special people."

Martha felt warm all the way down to her toes as she curled up next to Uncle Caleb in the big rocker. Uncle Caleb smoked and rocked as they watched Jeff create a face...a wonderful, frightening goblin.

"Meanest face I ever saw," judged Uncle Caleb.

"Most wonderful face I ever say," said Martha and she was looking straight at Uncle Caleb.

MOLLY

February 18, 1946. Virginia DiGregorio was 19, almost 20 years old.

Real life reference:

My mother had a real love of poetry, no wonder she referenced famous poets in her writing as well as screen stars and movies she enjoyed.

Johnny Whittier: An American poet and editor, John Greenleaf Whittier was born December 17, 1807, in Haverhill, Massachusetts. A Quaker devoted to social causes and reform, Whittier worked passionately for a series of abolitionist newspapers and magazines. Wikipedia

Longfellow: Henry Wadsworth Longfellow (February 27, 1807 – March 24, 1882) was an American poet and educator. Wikipedia

Boyer and Bacall: Screen stars circa 1945. Wikipedia

Ahab: Ahab was the seventh king of Israel since Jeroboam, the son and successor of King Omri and the husband of Jezebel of Sidon, according to the Hebrew Bible. Wikipedia

Cummings and Eliot: Edward Estlin "E. E." Cummings (October 14, 1894 – September 3, 1962), often styled as e e cummings, as he is attributed in many of his published works,[1] was an American poet, painter, essayist, author, and playwright. He wrote approximately 2,900 poems, two autobiographical novels, four plays, and several essays. Thomas Stearns Eliot OM (26 September 1888 – 4 January

1965) was an American-born British poet, essayist, publisher, playwright, literary critic, and editor. Wikipedia

Shelley: Percy Bysshe Shelley *(/bɪʃ/ (listen) BISH; 4 August 1792 – 8 July 1822) was one of the major English Romantic poets, widely regarded as one of the greatest lyrics and philosophical poets in the English language. Wikipedia*

Bryant: William Cullen Bryant *(November 3, 1794 – June 12, 1878) was an American romantic poet, journalist, and long-time editor of the New York Evening Post. Wikipedia*

Sign of the times:

"Confidential Agent": Confidential Agent is a *1945 American spy film starring Charles Boyer and Lauren Bacall which was a Warner Brothers production. Wikipedia*

Lady Esther and Lady Be Good cold cream: Lady Esther was the trademark of a cosmetic manufacturing company founded by German-born Syma Cohen and her siblings in Chicago in 1913 and operated as Lady Esther Company. It was incorporated in Illinois in 1922 and became America's top selling brand of cosmetics in the United States. Wikipedia   Note: Could not find a historical reference for "Lady Be Good Cold Cream".

Pill box hat: A pillbox hat is a small hat, usually worn by women, with a flat crown, straight, upright sides, and no brim. It is named after the small cylindrical or hexagonal cases that pills used to be sold in. Wikipedia

Lady in red (song by Louis Leo Prima):

Louis Leo Prima[3] was from a musical Italian American family in New Orleans, Louisiana. His father, Anthony Prima, was the son of Leonardo Di Prima, a Sicilian immigrant from Salaparuta, while his mother, Angelina Caravella, had immigrated from Ustica as a baby.[4] Prima was the second child of four; his older brother, Leon, was born in 1907, while his sisters Elizabeth and Marguerite were younger. Marguerite died when she was three years old. Leon, Louis, and Elizabeth were all baptized at St. Ann's Parish. They lived in a house at 1812 St.

Peter Street in New Orleans.[5]

Prima's mother was a music lover, she made sure that each child played an instrument. Louis was assigned the violin and started out playing at St. Ann's Parish.[5] He became interested in jazz when he heard black musicians, including Louis Armstrong. Local clubs such as Matranga's, Joe Segrettas, Tonti's Social Club, and Lala's Big 25 were all Italian-American clubs owned and operated by Italians in which African Americans frequently played and fraternized with Italians and Italian-Americans.[5]

New York was an attraction for hungry musicians during the Great Depression. It posed numerous risks, but all of the best artists in the nation made it in New York if not anywhere else. Guy Lombardo met Prima while he was performing at club Shim Sham during the Mardi Gras season of 1934.[5] In May 1935, Prima and Russell recorded "The Lady in Red", a national jukebox hit.

Counter stools in Drug stores

A soda shop, also often known as a malt shop (after malt), known as a "malted shop" in Canada, is a business akin to an ice cream parlor, and a drugstore soda fountain. Interiors were often furnished with a large mirror behind a marble counter with gooseneck soda spouts, plus spinning stools, round marble-topped tables, and wireframe sweetheart chairs. The counter-service soda fountain was introduced in 1903, and around that same time, drugstores began to attract noontime customers by adding sandwiches and light lunches. The beverage menu at a soda shop usually included ice cream sodas[1],[2] chocolate malts, fountain colas, and milkshakes. Wikiwand

Floorwalker

A floorwalker is a senior employee in a large store (usually a department store) who supervises sales staff, in addition to directing and assisting customers, answering any queries they may have.

Molly cry? Molly of counter 4, featuring Colgate's and other toothpastes, Maybelline that make you irresistible, Ponds, **Lady Esther and Lady Be Good cold cream,** powder base and self-drying cream base, Hot Tamale, Pinwheel, Keep Him Kissin', Red Red, purple tinges with blue and guaranteed to glow luminously in the dark lipstick, and brown, black, tan and ox-blood shoe polish? She didn't look like the type. Well, once Molly cried.

It wasn't the time she bounced down Main and Market caught in between cross sections of humanity bound for offices, schools, and only they knew what else, being tossed in the web like a spongy red ball, rolling gaily past furniture shops, meat markets and drug stores. It was in front of the drug store that the group of pint-sized kids looked at her and snickered. Then the tears could've come to her eyes when she forced herself to look in the full-length mirror of Stacy's Drugs, after she had entered the haven of its revolving doors to escape the pint-sized eyes and pint-sized snickers. There she stood – or rather there she bounced and rolled. Short and spongy, in red and pink. Funny how the buttons hadn't looked too brassy on the red hip-length coat when she bought the coat at a sale last pay day. Too much pink was showing below the red hem. And to climax the picture, a green, green feather shot straight up from the red **pillbox hat.** She blinked.

"The **Lady in red,** the fellows go crazy over the Lady in red." The old song shot through her mind. "The Lady in red, just these colors would knock you dead," she improvised and began to laugh. All the **counter stools** squeaked as the people sitting on them turned to look at the fat little lady in red laughing at herself in the middle of the **drugstore** floor. She looked like a bright poppy that had burst out of the flowered linoleum that was laid out, not too cleanly, on the floor.

How many of those people would have been surprised if they had known that under the bright colors and under the surface there was another Molly. A person different from the first Molly who snapped her gum while she chewed, who said "ain't" and was afraid of the **floorwalker** because he had had a year of business school. This other Molly wore beautiful clothes, spoke charmingly and was known to a great percentage of the American masses. She was everything beautiful. Long ago when the second Molly was just in the embryo stage of first Molly's dreams, the first Molly had come to the conclusion that everything beautiful must be found in poetry. For didn't every romantic heroine recite some lines of poetry. Didn't one of her teachers long ago in the first years of high school say that the most beautiful things were said in the most beautiful way in poetry? Poetry to Molly came to mean anything that rhymed to what book salesman told her were the best poems of the day. In her dreams behind the piles of lipstick and toothpaste of counter 4, fumbling, stuttering first Molly was transformed into the charming second Molly, poetess. And that was Molly's dream.

Lunch hours spent in bookstores were all too short, even though she swallowed hamburgers in double time so she would have a few extra minutes to browse around. Still always she had to run breathlessly, her arms filled with more poetry books from jingles to philosophical, to be behind her counter in time. Always the remarks from the counter girls working with her.

"Molly read poetry?" "What does she know about it?" They snickered. "Hey Molly, how's Johnny Whittier? Who spent the night with you? Longfellow? Look at her blush..." And so on.

Once, only once, Molly had confided to her counter-mate Lauren, how Shelley could thrill her as much as any True-Life story. Only Lauren couldn't see it that way. Just last week, after she had seen **"Confidential Agent"**, she had touched up her hair, put on tight skirts and changed her name to Lauren. Anything better than Boyer and Bacall? Molly was nutty. And she proceeded to let all the other counter-hands know. Everything boomeranged back to Molly. "Lady Molly" they called her. Working her way through college ---counter 4 was just a stop-off. The words burned like electric shots through her. Not for herself, but because those stupid change-pushers (Molly called them) had the nerve to make fun of her poets, the nerve to kick her books with their eyes. And she would cover them with paper from counter 4 and scurry home.

Home. A two-room home of a sofa convertible into a bed, a kitchenette that cried out for air when she squeezed her spongy self into it, and then, her bookshelf. Neat, immaculately clean, every book was a shining monument. Some women revered a nursery; Molly revered her bookshelf. Two bright candles burned on either side. Molly called them the inner lights that prompted the poets. Someday, half wishing, half afraid to whisper it, someday, perhaps they'd prompt her.

She'd show those other counter-girls. She used to bounce on a tall stool near the kitchen table, spearing olives with a tightly clenched fork. Her brows would sew themselves together and she'd plunge even harder with the fork when she thought of how she'd show everybody. She looked a little like Ahab sitting, body taut, on the stool, determined, half-mad, except that she harpooned olives while he harpooned whales.

One particular night the tiny flat was even more quiet than usual. Now and then the floors and walls creaked as though the burden of the heavy silence was too great for them. And Molly read. Pages and pages of Cummings and Eliot, which the salesman had assured her were made up of Real Poetry. Poor befuddled, bewildered Molly. Her signs mingled with the sighs of the floors, the walls, the chairs. Beautiful words strung along the page, line after line, but what did they mean? Longfellow she could understand. And Bryant. But these two. Minutes droned by as Molly struggled to understand, but then the beauty of the words, the phrases without meaning were too much for her and she was caught up into a whirl of verbs, nouns, adjectives---each more beautiful than the other; each becoming what she wanted it to become.

The end of the page. With an unconscious sigh, Molly raised glazed, feverish eyes to the tall candles burning, solemnly, faithfully for the unappreciative poets. Shelley, Cumming, Longfellow---if they could only know of this fiery, half - pagan, half-religious devotion. Tall, tall flames, cool and bright. Her eyes devoured them. Suddenly she was on her knees between the burning candles, clutching the book tightly. For an endless minute, she hypnotized the slender, cool flames with her eyes. They seemed to grow brighter, warmer from the fever in her gaze.

Just as suddenly, she rose and walked unsteadily towards a desk that faced the bookshelf. With her eyes still on the flames, she picked up a pencil and paper. This time she could write. This time she had been prompted. "They", the poets, through their burning inner lights had done it. She was sure now that the same light that had burned in Shelley, Longfellow was burning in her now waiting to be famed into a bright, bright flame.

What to write about? Night? She'd write about night---delicate night, ugly night. She could make anything whatever she wished. She was Aladdin and her lamp was the lead stub in her thick fingers. She, Molly, could be Aladdin. All she had to do was to move the magic stub up and down the paper carper. Thusly. Now. Delicately. Night as dark as. Maybelline. Stars shining, glittering like. Colgate's. Moon in clouds of. Ponds Cream. Ponds cream and red coats and alarm clocks and wrong change. And Maybelline nights and Colgate stars.

Aladdin and her lead stub. Frigid. The magic paper and stub as a sterile couple. Nothing came. Nothing.

Then Molly cried.

WEEKEND

Timeline:

May 22, 1946. Virginia DiGregorio was 19, almost 20 years old

Signs of the time:

Wanderer of the Wasteland: is a 1945 American Western film directed by Wallace Grissell and Edward Killy and starring James Warren in his RKO debut replacing Robert Mitchum who had starred in Nevada. Richard Martin, and Audrey Long also star in the film. Wikipedia

Real life reference:

Seems to refer to Wappingers Falls with the Main Street, movie theater, getting off at the bridge in the middle of town, up the street to The Park (which still exists today), white Park house (still there)

Did mom come back to Wappingers, her hometown, once a month?

Mom's middle name was Frances

St. Mary's Catholic Church in Wappingers Falls exists today, and the cornerstone of this structure was laid in 1877. "The bell was donated by the people of the parish in commemoration of the first mission held at St. Mary's by the Jesuit Fathers from May 25 through June 8, 1879." stmarywappingers.org/history

The trees on the side of the road had finally blossomed out since the last time four weeks ago when **Frances** had sat in this same bus and ridden down the South Road. She realized suddenly with a start that that was the reason why things looked so different this time. It seemed that for the first time in her life she was actually seeing trees---huge, spreading, dark. Now, with the darkening sky and the wet ground that made a swsh, swsh, swishing sound as the bus roared over it, the trees seemed too big and out of place. Out of season, really. They stretched out too far over the road, meeting leaf to leaf the trees bordering the other side of the highway, and meeting, they joined branches as though ready to press down and down until finally touching the concrete itself. And probably push and push until the earth swallows the road, thought Frances. She huddled closer in the corner of the seat and was glad that the driver had snapped off the lights of the bus when they left the city. There were too many people sitting around her whom she knew and to whom she didn't want to talk the dull, prying small talk of small-town acquaintances. A great many of them didn't recognize her. Only three years since she had left home, and she had come home on the average of once a month, but still the short years made a difference. Probably her new glasses and haircut helped, too.

At The Corners, the driver switched on the lights again. For a minute, the endless bumping and roaring of the bus stopped and a girl prepared to get off. Frances recognized her as Anne Botski. She's going to have a baby, she noticed. As though she had no control over her thoughts and almost as another person, Frances sat back and watched the pictures her mind flashed of Anne. Anne on a bike, long hair, blowing skirts---Anne picking flowers---Anne singing in the choir---Anne who had been her ideal. Yet as Anne passed Frances on her way up the aisle towards the door, neither of them had spoken. She who had seemed so young, so popular and glamorous to Frances three years ago was now only a tired, dumpy-looking woman who was going to have a baby. And now Frances was the gay girl, the young girl, the glamorous. This was her day.

The sight of the bell tower of **St. Mary's** made her realize that she was almost home. Just a while more, down the wet streets---the Knights of Columbus Hall, Judy's Ice Cream Parlor, the Jew's grocery store, the movie-house. **"Wanderer of the Wasteland"**, was playing. Frances got off at the bridge, aided by a dozen pairs of scrutinizing eyes that remained on the bus to be carried up Main Street and then home. There was water under the bridge. There should be. It had rained all weekend and the water ran and fell with such force that big, wet drops sprayed all around Frances who was standing looking over the thick bridge wall.

As she passed the bakery shop, Frances saw Mildred and Betty, the two counter-girls, drop their work and saunter to the window to see who the person was with the suitcase. The fellows in the restaurant across the street stared more openly. The "hellos" from all of them were weak, short and small-town-ish in their pretended sincerity and obvious questioning and hypocrisy. Frances wondered now why she hadn't remained on the bus till she reached the top of the hill that was Main Street. It would've eliminated the necessity of making a liar and hypocrite of herself---if not the other people. At least, she wouldn't had had to answer their short smiles with a shorter one of her own.

The Park was her haven. As soon as she reached one of the paths that screened her from the rest of the town, she stopped and put down her suitcase. Then she took off her hat and for a minute or two just stood there, letting the damp air of the valley seep into her hair, her eyes. She breathed it in in long, slow breaths and tasted the dampness on her lips. She felt suddenly very small and powerless under the great massiveness of the pine trees. Yet with all their size and strength, they were graceful, mysterious. Some dark sky showed in an opening through the dark branches. Gazing at that opening, seven years suddenly slipped by and Frances was again the small girl coming home alone from school, running up the four concrete steps leading to the widest path in the park, running extra fast because in her child's mind she was creating fantastic horrors of men hiding behind trees waiting to pounce on little girls. One night Frances had forgotten to run, forgotten to create fantastic horrors. Later all she was able to remember was that there was a huge, graceful, dark pine tree whose branches stretched so high that it had hurt her neck to tip her head back so far to see their tops. Through an opening in the dark branches was showing a dark piece of sky. And Frances felt a tremendous sweep as though on the branches had reached down and pulled her soul, up, up to the opening. From that height her soul had heard a pebble shift in the sands, had felt a cloud brush against a leaf, had tasted the lips of all the lovers in the world, had seen a wild wave embrace a barren shore. Her reckless, youthful soul, crying out to deaf ears, made the dark opening suddenly golden with light. Then down, down, down. There remained on the dark opening, a terrible silence and a terrible silence and a vast sense of something lost, something lonely, a tremendous space that had to be filled, but with what? A longing that in that instant Frances had known could never be filled. All she was able to see then were faces behind the dark trees, faces of men waiting to pounce on little girls. She had raced down the path, past the big, white Park House, down the middle of the road. A frightened child running home late from school.

As she started up the back steps at a slower rate of speed, she had heard her mother's and brother's voiced raised, angry in argument. Frances didn't want to go in then. Before as she had raced down the road, her heart beating so fast, she had felt that she had to sell someone this new feeling she had had in the Park. She had to have someone filling the empty space, the longing, right then or else it would grow and grow. She opened the door and walked in. When she closed the door, she knew she had closed out the trees, the Park, her soul.

Later she had heard her father talk to the oldest boy. Pat

who had come home from the West to visit. Pat was different from the rest of the family. He swore more, drank, said to hell with the world. He didn't live in the world; the world lived in him. That's why he couldn't live in a small town, because in a small town you couldn't live life by mouthfuls and by taking more than you could chew. Here the people poured out life to you, by the teaspoons. Pat was too big; he was almost starving on the rations and so one night he had gone out and swallowed a big hunk of life. Frances worshipped him for it, envied him that he could do it. But her father, watching the pious people screw their mouths, cross themselves and talk through decaying lips spoke to Pat and said,

"This is our world; we have to live it. We can't do like you, come back and leave it on and off."

She had seen her family for the first time that night, as they really were. And she knew then that they could never help her. Slowly at first, then with more certainty, she saw in their eyes a dark opening, a terrible silence, and a vast sense of something lost, something lonely. And through it all a whispering undercurrent of unrest, discontent, frustration. None of them could run; this was their world. Frances had felt very old. Someday before the dark opening came to be clearly seen in her eyes, she had to run. Someday, while the dark opening still remained, just the dark sky showing through dark branches in a park. Someday, before she would have to say –this is my world; I have to live in it.

The years slipped back into place. Frances lost sight of the opening in the branches as the sky and trees and night blended into one even darkness. The damp air from the valley gave her a chill; it made her hair feel dirty and sticky. As she breathed it inside, she felt a terrible silence and a vast sense of loss, of loneliness, of longing. She picked up her suitcase and walked down the path, past the big, white Park House and down the middle of the road. Her steps were stumbly, hurried, as though she wished to run. But it wouldn't look right for a lady all dressed up and carrying a suitcase to go running down the middle of the road. For a child running home late from school it would be different.

VIDA

Timeline:

May 8, 1946. Virginia DiGregorio was 19, almost 20 years old.

Sign of the times:

Ordinary black disk with red in the center (78 vinyl record): A phonograph record (also known as a gramophone record, especially in British English), or simply a record, is an analog sound storage medium in the form of a flat disc with an inscribed, modulated spiral groove. The groove usually starts near the periphery and ends near the center of the disc. At first, the discs were commonly made from shellac; starting in the 1940s polyvinyl chloride became common, hence the name vinyl. Wikipedia

I t was thundering. First a big roll like lots and lots of men's voices talking all at once, then an ear-splitting bang, as though one man a little more important that the rest had clapped his huge hands together for quiet. The quiet rolled louder than the thunder, all over the big yard, against the house, through the shut windows; it knocked against the walls, the curtains, against the ears of the ten year old child standing motionlessly, hands hanging limp, before the rain-soaked window. She seemed not to notice the water sliding to the outside sill; the lightning which made the man and woman in the next room jump with fright performed before the un-reacting, unappreciative eyes of a ten-year-old child. In reality, the child appeared to be unconscious of all that was happening. Unconscious of all but the rolls of thunder which became more and more frequent, more and more loud. A sudden flash of lightning followed by the clash of rolling voices showed an odd, half-smile on the otherwise blank face.

The first real signs of dark had appeared when Vida's mother found her standing, half-smiling, before the still rain-soaked window. Even while the mother undressed and washed the child, the dull eyes stared unseeing at all the motions. Only the half-smile that appeared when the thunder knocked on the bedroom windows was proof of life in the strange, little body. Once she laughed, a laugh that excluded her mother, the bed, the chairs, the obviously expensive doll in the tiny rocker.

For two days it rained. Two more days Vida stood watching and listening, half-smiling, before the same rain-soaked window, hands limp, eyes unseeing, her ears the only living part of her. Tall Dr. Brief assured the mother that it was merely an infatuation. Vida was, he said so delicately---different from other children. Her small body had never really begun to grow and somehow, unfortunately, but---who could do anything about it? Her mind--- you know, retarded growth, perhaps when she was older, proper training. How many times had tall Dr. Brief and the mother stood in the other room and talked about Vida. Humor her. The next night when Vida laughed at the knocking thunder, the mother laughed too and called it "a pretty noise". Vida only heard the rattling windows.

When the storm stopped, Vida had to be led from the no longer rain-soaked window. She stood where her mother placed her, of if she had been made to sit down, she sat, every organ as alive as those of the expensive doll in the tiny rocker. Not even her ears listened any longer. Tall Dr. Brief and the mother again whispered in the other room. Get her out of it---make her respond---something to interest her. And the mother could only say---her eyes, so dull.

No one quite knew when the record came to be so important to Vida, except that one day the mother found her standing before the dining room table staring, staring at an **ordinary black disk with red in the center.** What had the doctor said? An interest---make her respond. The mother grasped the disk, not even looking at what title was written in the red center and placed in in the record machine. Vida's eyes never left off staring at the now empty space where the record had been. The disk played to the wall, the ears of the mother, the soft curtains. It wasn't until the second

Boomlay, boomlay, boomlay, BOOM

that Vida began to half-smile. When the record called

Boom, steal the pygmies,

Boom, kill the Arabs,

Boom, kill the white men

Vida laughed. A laugh that excluded her mother, the soft curtains, the walls.

For a week, the record called over and over. For a week Vida stood motionless, watching, and listening, half-smiling, before the fast-revolving disk, hands limp, eyes unseeing, her ears the only living part of her. When the needle reached the edge of the disk, Vida waited unmoving until the automatic hand began its journey across the revolving blackness. In the other room tall Dr. Brief rubbed his hands, smiled---interest, amazing, maybe results. The next time Vida laughed; the mother laughed with her. Vida only heard the click of the automatic hand beginning a fresh journey.

Two weeks later the mother talked in the other room--- same record over and over---despised Congo---take it from Vida. Tall Dr. Bried looked concerned, rubbed his hands---uh, maybe--- shock---might bring response. Yes, take the record away from Vida.

That night the thunder knocked outside the window; the

record called from the inside. Vida laughed. Before the automatic hand could resume its well-worn path around the blackness, the mother reached with cold hands towards the record. She held it close to her as she faced Vida. It didn't look smooth on top when it wasn't going around and around. She began to talk---record business nonsense, hadn't she heard enough? Tall Dr. Brief had said Vida needed to respond. Respond, Vida, respond.

The automatic hand wasn't going any more. The record had stopped calling. The soft curtains, the walls, the mother heard the stillness. They heard the water slide down the shut window onto the outside sill and drop heavily on a blade of grass; the thunder knocked on the window. They heard a child hesitantly turn to face the knocks, heard her hands limply brush the air. They heard a door shut between them and her as they heard Vida throw back her head and laugh.

ACKNOWLEDGEMENT

This book was lovingly compiled by Carla Villarreal and Luke Rollins, Virginia Rollins' grandson.

The final part of the story 'Bully at the Bus Stop' was completed by David Rollins, son of Virginia Rollins.

ABOUT THE AUTHOR

Virginia Rollins

Virginia Rollins was born in 1926, the youngest of four children, to Antonio and Maria DiGregorio. Growing up in an immigrant family in the small town of Wappingers Falls, New York, her early life spanned both World War II and the Great Depression.

Virginia graduated early from high school, earned a Bachelor of Science degree from SUNY Albany and an MS in Spanish from Middlebury College in VT. By her early 20's she was teaching at Manhasset High School in New York where her career spanned 30 years.

It was in Manhasset that she met her husband Dwight and had four children. Virginia currently has 13 grandchildren, 6 great grandchildren with one more on the way.

Virginia devoted herself to her husband and children, and secondly to her teaching career. Known as the encourager, the motivator, the communicator, she was blessed with the gift of listening and discerning.

After retirement she moved to Virginia and is currently in Winchester at Westminster Canterbury.

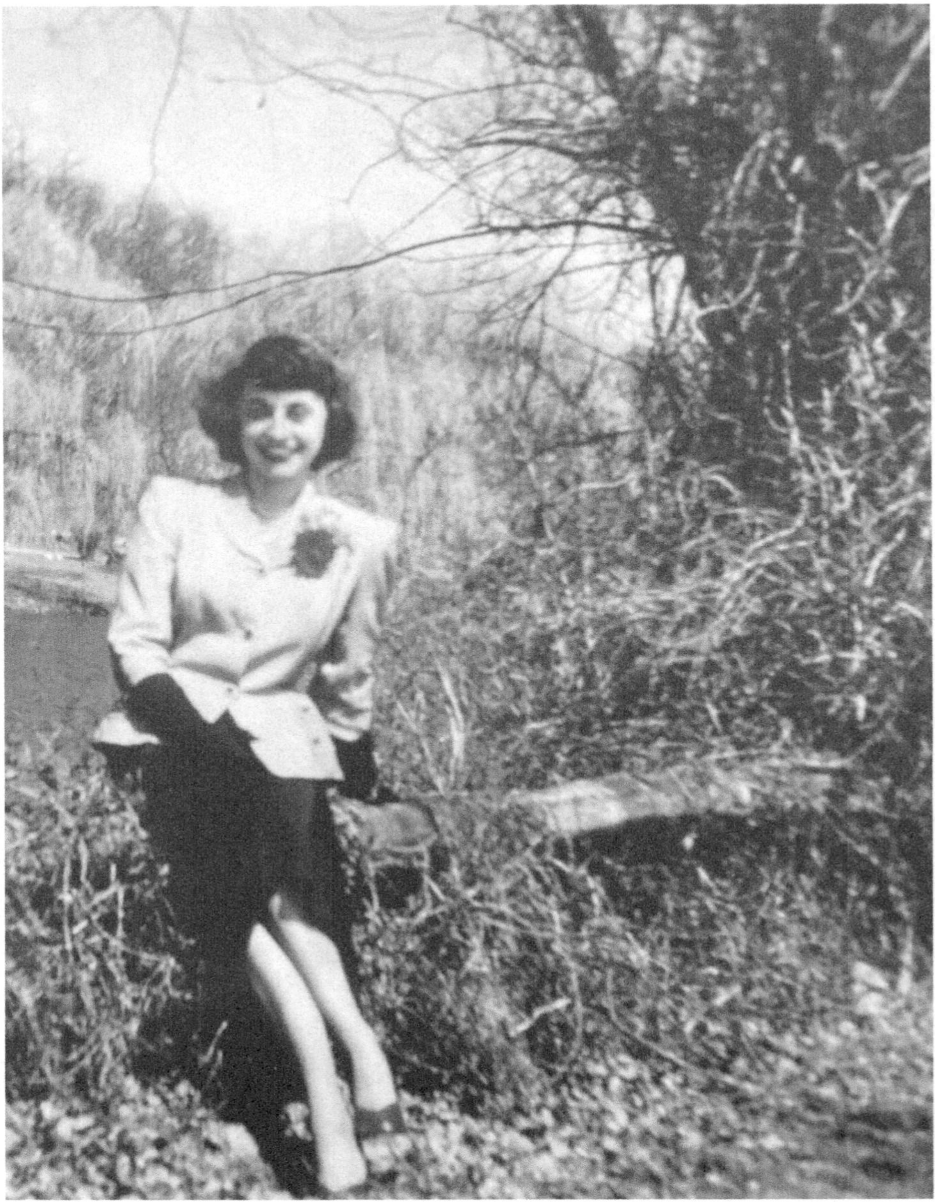

Loaded Birch

Dawd = done

When small me. Blac
took my grandfathe

Saturday Morning, Spr

Ten o'clock. She s
around corners and
sprawl out over the
between the two ho
really should no
there at all.
ye without fir
rain road,
fore proceed
les and
ta
s in
he

Di Gregorio, Virginia
Er. 110 c
Feb. 18, 1946

Made in the USA
Middletown, DE
03 October 2020

20658613R00086